She's Got the Beat

How Not to Spend Your Senior Year
BY CAMERON DOKEY

Royally Jacked
BY NIKI BURNHAM

Ripped at the Seams
BY NANCY KRULIK

Spin Control
BY NIKI BURNHAM

Cupidity
BY CAROLINE GOODE

South Beach Sizzle
BY SUZANNE WEYN AND DIANA GONZALEZ

She's Got the Beat
BY NANCY KRULIK

She's Got the Beat

NANCY KRULIK

Simon Pulse
New York London Toronto Sydney

SIMON PULSE
An imprint of Simon & Schuster
Children's Publishing Division
1230 Avenue of the Americas, New York, NY 10020

Copyright © 2005 by Nancy Krulik
All rights reserved, including the right of reproduction in whole or in part in any form.

SIMON PULSE and colophon are registered trademarks of Simon & Schuster, Inc.

Designed by Ann Zeak
The text of this book was set in Garamond 3.

Manufactured in the United States of America
First Simon Pulse edition April 2005
10 9 8 7 6 5 4
Library of Congress Control Number 2004112750
ISBN: 978-1-4424-1419-8

For Danny,
the drummer in our house

She's Got
the Beat

One

"And so, as we move on past our high school years . . ."

Miranda Lockheart shut her lips tight and fought back a yawn as the class valedictorian continued his endless speech. The hot Texas sun was beating down on her head, and the small, square, navy-blue graduation hat did little to shade her eyes. She'd have given anything to get out of her long, heavy robe right then. Who the hell had had the bright idea of getting polyester robes for an outdoor Texas graduation, anyway? All Miranda could think about was slipping on her swimsuit and taking a dip in the pool at her best friend Cally

Morton's house. But that would have to wait until after the ceremony, at the big graduation party.

"This is endless," Cally whispered into Miranda's ear. "You would have definitely given a better speech than Keith Lerner. Man, he sure loves the sound of his own voice."

Miranda shrugged and tucked a strand of her long, wheat-colored hair behind her ear. She didn't know if her speech would have been better if she'd been the valedictorian, but it sure as shootin' would've been shorter. But she wasn't the valedictorian. She'd been close—only .4 percentage points separated her final cum from Keith's. But he'd won the valedictorian spot. And that meant the whole class was going to have to suffer through his speech.

Actually, not *everyone* was suffering. Denny Callahan, Miranda's boyfriend, was actually having a great time at graduation. Of course that probably had something to do with the fact that he and his buddy Carson Smith were taking hearty swigs off a bottle of Jack Daniel's that Carson had swiped from his daddy's bar.

"You want a sip, Rand?" Denny whispered in Miranda's ear.

Miranda shook her head. "Put that thing away, Denny," she warned him. "You're going to get us all in trouble."

"Oh, come on," Denny groaned. "I couldn't graduate without my old buddy JD, now could I? He and I have shared a lot of good times together senior year." He took another hit from the bottle.

"*You* almost didn't graduate at all," Carson teased his buddy. "You're just lucky Mr. Dobson raised your trig grade to a C minus instead of a D plus."

"It wasn't luck," Denny boasted. "It was skill. And talent."

"You mean you actually *studied* for the final?" Carson was incredulous.

Denny shook his head. "Nah. I just knew exactly how to make old man Dobson so crazy that he didn't want to risk having me in his math class for summer school. He passed me just to get rid of me."

Miranda sighed. She didn't doubt it for a minute. Denny wasn't exactly Einstein. But he was so damned cute, with his strawberry blond hair that curled just a little bit at the edges, and those hazel, puppy dog eyes. He was really sweet, in his own down-home way. There wasn't anything in the world he wouldn't have done for Miranda. She could always count on him. That meant a lot.

Besides, Denny wasn't going to need a big fancy college education. He was going into his father's cattle feed business. He'd wind up a rich businessman like his daddy no matter what happened. Still, Mr. Callahan *had* insisted his son get some kind of education after high school. So Denny was going to County Community in the fall, to get an associate's degree in business. He was also going to work part-time at Callahan Feed, starting with a job in the delivery department. Mr. Callahan had a theory that his son should get to know all aspects of the business from the bottom up.

The thought of Denny going to college right here in Barton brought a cloud of melancholy over Miranda. She'd known all year that she and Denny would be separated as soon as school was over, but she'd managed to block it out of her mind. Lately, there'd been so much to keep her from thinking about it: prom, the year-book-signing party, final exams. But now, here it was, graduation, and there was no putting it off any further. In two weeks, Miranda would be heading off to Austin, ready to start as a freshman at Lone Star State.

Miranda had hoped that she could start school in the fall like her friends. That would have given her one last lazy summer with Denny. But Lone Star State College had given her a partial scholarship on the condition that she take a precalculus course over the summer, so that she'd be at the same level as all their other incoming freshmen in the fall. Miranda wasn't a great lover of math. She'd managed to keep her high cum by not taking any math her senior year, and instead piling on the English electives. But as much as the admissions department of Lone Star State had been impressed with her literary studies, they'd still insisted on the summer math course. And Miranda couldn't afford to say no. Unlike the Callahans, the Lockheart family wasn't rich. Miranda's dad owned a nursery just outside of Barton. He sold plants and trees and the like to local families. He made a decent living, but not enough to put his only daughter through college on his own. Miranda needed that partial scholarship. It was why she'd worked so hard all through high school.

"Hey, you think Ross really took the bet?" Denny asked Carson, interrupting Miranda's thoughts.

"What bet?" Cally whispered, grabbing the bottle of Jack Daniel's from Carson and taking a big swig.

"I bet him ten bucks he'd be too chicken to go nude to graduation," Carson said, and laughed. "He said he'd do it. Imagine him naked at graduation. What a jerk."

"*You're* the jerk," Cally told him. "We're all wearing these long robes. How are you going to know if he took the bet? Did you suddenly develop X-ray vision?"

"She's got you there, dude," Denny guffawed.

Carson frowned. He obviously hadn't considered that.

"Will you guys shut up?" Miranda warned. "Mr. Douglas is about to start handing out the diplomas." A feeling of both nervousness and excitement took over her body. This was it: the end of her high school career, and the beginning of . . . well, Miranda wasn't exactly sure about that.

"John Taylor Brewer . . . Marie Pamela Buskin . . . Dennis Lawrence Callahan . . ." Mr. Douglas read into the microphone.

"That's me!" Denny exclaimed, leaping out of his chair and moving toward the aisle. He stopped and gave Miranda a huge kiss as he passed, sliding his tongue wickedly past her lips and deep into her mouth. She flinched slightly as the taste of Jack Daniel's passed from his tongue to hers. Then she blushed, realizing half the senior class had been looking in their direction.

"Ross Darnell . . . Lila Mae Denton . . . Anna Douglas," the school principal continued to read the names of the graduates out loud.

"Whoa," Cally exclaimed, reaching her hand up to hold on to her hat as a strong wind began to blow across the football field. "That sure came out of nowhere."

Miranda blinked as the dirt kicked up. "I hope this doesn't mean rain," she said, holding on to her hat as well. Her long blond hair whipped around her face, blinding her for a second.

"Oh, my GOD!" Cally shouted. "I don't believe it."

"What?" Miranda said. She followed the direction of Cally's glance. She was looking up at the stage, where Denny, Ross, and Lila Mae were already standing, their robes blowing wildly around them. Suddenly, Carter didn't need X-ray vision. Thanks to the wind, everyone could see that Ross had taken him up on his bet. The entire graduating class, and their invited guests, had just gotten a full-frontal view of Ross's most prized possessions: *the Darnell family jewels!*

"Guess you're out ten bucks," Cally informed Carter.

Miranda shook her head. "His parents are going to kill him," she remarked as she watched Ross struggle to hold down his graduation gown.

"Good thing I'm not having a weenie roast at the party tonight," Cally added.

"Wouldn't want Ross to get that thing too close to the grill!" She and Carson burst into a fit of hysterics.

"You guys, stop it," Miranda said, giggling despite the fact that she felt really awful for Ross. And she continued laughing, even as the principal handed her a diploma and proudly proclaimed that Miranda Lockheart was now a graduate of Barton High School, class of 2005.

"I think this is the best party you've ever thrown, Cal," Miranda declared, plopping herself down on one of the lawn chairs in Cally's huge backyard. She took a huge bite of one of the ribs on her plate, and then wiped the sauce from her chin with a napkin. "I'm sure going to miss barbecue like this."

"They have ribs in Austin, too," Cally assured her. "It's only about four hours away, you know."

"May as well be four *hundred* hours," Miranda groused. "Without a car, I'll never get home. Besides, forget the barbecue. *You're* going to school all the way in L.A. When am I ever going to see you?"

"Thanksgiving, Christmas. Next summer. Anyhow, we'll talk. That's what the phone's for. I think between us we can figure out the time difference."

Miranda sighed and said nothing. She didn't have to. The look in her eyes said it all. She was watching as Denny leaped off the diving board and did a flip into Cally's swimming pool.

"He'll visit you," Cally assured her. "He'll probably be up in Austin all the time. He's crazy about you. Always has been, ever since we were kids."

"Not crazy enough to have tried to get into Lone Star with me," Miranda moaned. She frowned. This was a particularly sore point with her. "I told him, if he could just work a little harder . . ."

Cally shook her head. "He's not a college kind of guy, Rand. You know that. And he sure as hell wouldn't be happy in a big city like Austin. He's a Barton boy born and bred, like his dad. He's comfortable here."

"I am too," Miranda said, and sighed.

"Yeah," Cally agreed. "For now. But you and I are meant for other things. We have different goals from Denny's."

"Goals?" Miranda asked her. "I don't have any goals. Hell, I'm leaving for college in a few days and I don't even have a major yet."

"You'll declare one," Cally assured her.

"Easy for you to say, Miss UCLA film school. You'll be winning Oscars before you're twenty-five. But me . . ."

"You've got lots of talents, Rand. You just have to find the one that you want to dedicate your life to. That's why you're going to college. To figure things out."

Miranda nodded. "I guess. But it sure would be easier to have the whole thing mapped out like Denny does, you know?"

"*Easier*, sure," Cally agreed. "But not nearly as much fun." She smiled at her best friend. "There's no meat left on that rib. You're gnawing on the bone. You want another one?"

"Sure, why not?" Cally said. She stood up from the lounge chair, brushed a few corn bread crumbs from her shorts, and headed over to the huge spread Cally's parents had set out underneath a tent on the south side of the lawn. But before she could reach the table, Denny ran up, grabbed her from behind, and hugged her tight.

"Hey, Rand!" he greeted her, turning her around and planting a big kiss on her lips.

"Denny! You're getting me all wet," she said, jumping away. A few of the boys started to snicker. Miranda blushed, realizing they'd taken her seemingly innocent statement in a decidedly un-innocent way. "Oh, grow up!" Miranda shouted at Carter and the other guys standing behind Denny. But that just made the boys in her graduating class laugh harder. Of course, it didn't help matters that most of them were pretty drunk. Cally's parents had provided plenty of lemonade and iced tea, the unofficial drinks of Texas. But the guys had brought some of their own refreshments. Suffice to say their lemonade was a lot harder than what Miranda had been drinking.

Denny reached out and grabbed Miranda again, pulling her body even closer to his than before. She could feel his heart beating hard, and smell the chlorine on his skin. She smiled at him, reached up, and brushed one of his strawberry blond curls from his forehead. He grinned back at her, wrinkling his face so that the line of freckles across the bridge of his nose all but disappeared. For a moment, Miranda forgot that there was anyone else in the Mortons' yard besides the two of them.

How was she ever going to leave this guy?

Apparently, Denny was thinking the same thing, because at that very moment he let go of Miranda, dropped to the ground on one knee, and took her hand in his. She looked at him strangely, confused. What was Denny up to?

And then, in a split second, it became abundantly clear: Denny was going to propose to her—right here, in the middle of Cally's yard, with all these people around.

But first, he was going to have to get his balance. A full day of Jack Daniel's, hot Texas sun, and heavy-duty partying had left Denny a little shaky. He teetered from side to side on his knee. At one point he almost toppled over, and Miranda had to use her left hand to hold him upright.

"Thanks," he murmured. "See, that's why I can't let you go to Austin. Who'd hold me up when I'm fallin' down?"

"Come on, Denny," Miranda whispered. "Get up."

"Uh-uh," Denny told her. "Not till I ask you something."

"Den, not here. . . ."

But Denny would not be dissuaded. "Miranda Lockheart, would you do me the horror of—"

"I think you mean *honor* of, buddy," Carter interrupted him.

"Right," Denny said, and gave out a little drunken laugh. "I mean, will you do me the *honor* of becoming my wife?"

Miranda stared at him for a minute, certain that he was joking. This had to be one of Denny's ridiculous theatrical stunts—an attention-getting moment like the ones he'd pulled all through school.

But the look in Denny's eyes wasn't filled with teasing laughter. It was more an expression of drunken desperation. He really was proposing. He really wanted her to stay with him. *To share his life with him.*

Miranda's mind raced. *Not now, Denny.* Not right before she was about to leave for Austin. It wasn't fair. He knew it wouldn't take much to make her stay here, where it was safe. It would be so easy to move in with Denny, who loved her and would be able to take care of her. She would be able to stay in Barton and have her whole life planned out. It was comfortable here. And Denny could give her everything she wanted: a home, children, security. And he'd do it gladly, because he loved her.

Besides, she could go to college here. *Community* college, just like Denny. Who said she needed a four-year school? There were plenty of things you could do with an associate's degree. She wouldn't have to have some sort of big career. She wasn't seeking fame and fortune, like Cally. What was wrong with just being Mrs. Denny Callahan?

Mrs. Denny Callahan. She'd written it on her notebook a million times since ninth grade, when she and Denny had started going out. And now it could be her name, for real.

Everyone was quiet now, waiting to see how this would play out. There was only one thing Miranda could say. She had to tell him what was in her heart. "I'm sorry, Denny."

★

Miranda was never sure what the expression on Denny's face was like after that moment, because she never looked back. Instead, she dropped his hand, turned, and ran off into the night, toward a future of complete and utter uncertainty.

TWO

On Monday morning, just two weeks after she'd graduated from high school, Miranda stepped out of the bus station in Austin. She pulled down the front of her Stetson to shield her eyes from the blinding sunlight. Austin in June was stiflingly hot, and the bright sunlight reflecting off the sidewalk just made things worse.

She headed over to take her place in the taxi line. Taking a cab to the Lone Star State College housing office was a luxury she could ill afford. But at the moment it was her only option. Miranda had been to Austin only twice before—both times to visit the college—and she didn't know the layout of the city at all. She didn't relish the idea of being lost in the heat while dragging two heavy suitcases.

"Howdy," the cab driver greeted her as he helped her place her suitcases in the trunk of the taxi. "Where can I take you?"

Miranda read him the address of the housing office, and then leaned back into the worn leather seat of the cab. She looked out the window at the city that was her new home. As the driver moved through the downtown area, she noticed lots of teenagers like herself, relaxing in sidewalk cafés, walking in and out of clothing boutiques, and hanging out near art galleries. It was a funky neighborhood, and Miranda made a mental note of the streets, as she was certain she'd want to visit this part of town again—especially the big music store, Waterloo Records. Of course, she'd have to wait until her father shipped her stereo equipment up to her dorm room before she went there. It was too much for her to carry on the bus.

Miranda sighed a bit, thinking about her father. Her parents had really wanted to drive her up to Austin to get her settled in.

But summer was a busy season for them, and they'd found it impossible to delay landscaping the golf course for even a day. So Miranda had had to settle for a big, weepy good-bye scene at the bus station.

Cally had come with the Lockhearts to see Miranda off. She'd vowed to call often with all the news from the homefront, but even still, saying good-bye to Cally had been really hard.

Saying good-bye to Denny, on the other hand, hadn't been difficult at all, since he hadn't come to the bus station. He hadn't taken any of her calls or returned her messages either. It had been two weeks since the disastrous graduation party, and Denny had obviously taken her refusal of his marriage proposal as a signal that the relationship was completely over.

But that hadn't been how Miranda had wanted things to wind up. Why did it have to be his way or the highway? Why couldn't things have continued as they'd planned—a long-distance romance, one in which Denny would come to visit her in Austin, and she would see him at home in Barton on holidays?

Of course, deep down, Miranda knew the answer to that. Denny was a proud guy. He'd been shamed in front of all his friends. It was something he'd probably never forgive her for.

But there wasn't much else Miranda could have done. She didn't want to marry Denny—at least not now. Not before she'd found out what she was good at; where her talents lay. She didn't want to spend her whole life wondering *what if.*

"Okay, this is it," the cab driver said, pulling the taxi over in front of a large white building. "You need help with those bags?"

"No thanks, I can handle them," Miranda assured him. She paid the driver the amount on the meter, and then quickly figured out a 10 percent tip, just as her father had reminded her to. Then she got out of the cab, took her bags from the trunk, and headed up the stairs.

"Can I help you?" a college student at the front desk of the undergraduate housing office asked Miranda.

Miranda stared at her for a moment. She'd never met anyone quite like this girl before. She was really tall, at least six feet, and she had a series of silver hoops going up each of her ears. The hoops in her ears matched the one that was slid through a hole in her right eyebrow. She had a large tattoo of the sun on her left shoulder, and her eyes were circled with more black eyeliner than Miranda had ever seen anyone wear before.

"Hello?" the girl said, waving her hand in front of Miranda's face.

"What? Oh. I'm sorry. I guess I'm just a little overwhelmed."

The girl behind the desk took an observant glance at Miranda's cleanly scrubbed face, long blond ponytail, jeans and cowboy hat, and laughed. "Don't worry," she told her. "They're not all like me."

Miranda blushed. "Oh, I didn't . . ."

"Don't sweat it." The girl stuck out her hand. "I'm Kathleen. I'm a sophomore at Lone Star. This summer I'm the work-study intern in the housing department. And you are . . . ?"

"Miranda Lockheart. I'm here to get my housing assignment."

"For the fall?" Kathleen asked her.

"Boy, you sure aren't a procrastinater."

"Actually, I'm starting classes tomorrow. I have to take precalculus."

Kathleen looked at her strangely. "There are no room assignments for the summer. The dorms are closed until September. Except, of course, to the football team. They get to use them when practice starts in August." For some reason that seemed to annoy her immensely.

"But I sent in the forms, and they told me that there would be a room for me when I began my freshman year," Miranda stammered. She blinked her eyes a few times as the tears began to form. Here she was in a strange city, where she didn't know a soul, and this girl was telling her she had no place to live. "I brought a check with me and everything and—"

"Oh God, don't cry," Kathleen urged, handing her a purple tissue from her desk.

"But they promised me . . ."

"Yes. I know, for your freshman year. Unfortunately, that doesn't start until September. The class you're taking this summer is only four credits. That means you won't be an actual full-time, matriculated freshman student until September, when your sixteen-credit schedule begins."

Now there was no holding the tears back. They just streamed out. Miranda had never been on her own before. She'd never had to handle any kind of emergency without her parents to help. Now here she was, faced with homelessness, which was a MAJOR emergency, and she was completely on her own. She had no idea what to do.

"Here, sit down," Kathleen said, offering Miranda her desk chair. "I'll get you a glass of water."

As Kathleen walked over to the water cooler, Miranda wiped her eyes with the purple tissue, and tried to catch her breath.

"Actually, I do know of *one* place where you can get a room for the summer," Kathleen said, returning with a small paper cup of cool water. "It's not officially a dorm, but—"

"Really?" Miranda said, brightening.

·Kathleen nodded. "My roommate and I have been looking for someone to take the extra room in our house. It's right off campus. There's a bus that stops on our corner that could get you here in fifteen minutes. A lot of Lone Star students live in our neighborhood."

Miranda thought for a moment. An off-campus house with two other students. And if Kathleen's roommate was anything like Kathleen . . . well, it definitely wasn't what her parents had had in mind. On the other hand, they hadn't exactly had *homelessness* in mind either.

"Why don't you just come and take a look at the place?" Kathleen suggested. "We could go over there now. I was just about to take my break, anyway."

"Okay," Miranda said quietly. "Thank you."

"No problem," Kathleen assured her. "If you take the room, you'll be doing us a favor. It's a lot easier splitting the rent three ways instead of two."

"Well, here we are, home sweet home," Kathleen said as she carried one of Miranda's two suitcases up the steps of her house.

Miranda tried not to act too disappointed as she stepped up onto the old wooden porch. But it wasn't easy. The house was in pretty bad shape. It tilted more than slightly to one side. The floorboards on the porch were coming up in places, and the old glider was missing one of its cushions.

Kathleen jiggled the front lock with her key and opened the door. "Come on in," she said, standing aside to let Miranda enter first.

The door opened into an old, wood-paneled living room. There was a well-worn brown couch pressed up against the wall and two beanbag chairs on the floor. On the wall opposite the couch, a series of plastic milk crates had been stacked to make bookshelves. An old TV rested on top of a stack of cinder blocks.

Sitting on the couch, completely engrossed in a soap opera on the TV, was a redhead wearing a frilly short nightgown.

"Hey Miss, this is Miranda," Kathleen introduced her. "She's going to be a freshman in the fall. Miranda, this is Missy. She's the one I share the house with."

"It's just the two of you in this big house?" Miranda asked.

Kathleen shook her head. "Oh no. There's also Mother."

Miranda looked at Kathleen strangely. "You live with your *mother?*"

Kathleen laughed. "Not exactly," she said.

"Mother's that mannequin over there," Missy explained, without lifting her eyes from the TV. "Kathleen picked her up at a yard sale."

"She's kind of our mascot," Kathleen explained. "Hey, who gave her the hat? Nice touch."

Miranda looked toward the corner of the room. Sure enough there was a mannequin standing there. She was dressed in an odd assortment of clothes: a torn flamenco skirt, an old black sweater with a fake-fur collar, and a half-crushed satiny top hat. A black patent leather pocketbook was slung over one arm.

"Mother watches over us." Kathleen joked. "We wouldn't want to be living here *unsupervised.*"

Missy laughed. "You want an iced tea?" she asked, getting up from the couch. "I'm going for a refill."

"That would be nice," Miranda said. "Thank you."

"Have a seat," Kathleen suggested, pointing to one of the beanbag chairs as Missy walked out of the room to get the drinks.

Miranda sank into the vinyl chair, suddenly realizing how tired she was. "Oh, these are very comfortable," she said, sighing.

"Our old roomie, Amy, donated them to the cause when she graduated a couple of weeks ago," Kathleen told her. "She also left us all her pots and pans. Not that Missy or I ever do a whole lot of cooking."

"How come you're here now, if you're an incoming freshman?" Missy asked as she reentered the room with the tea.

"Our guest's taking precalc this summer," Kathleen told her, "but there're no dorm rooms open. So she needs a place to stay."

"Just until school starts in the fall," Miranda clarified the situation.

Kathleen shrugged. "You're not tied to the dorms," she told Miranda. "You could just stay here if you like it."

"I didn't plan on living in an off-campus place either," Missy told her. "Neither did Kathleen. But here we are. What can I say? Kat and I are just campus-housing misfits."

"Speak for yourself," Kathleen argued. "Mother and I fit this place perfectly."

"Well, I came here because I didn't have anyplace else to live," Missy said, and sighed.

"She got thrown out of her sorority house for starting a mutiny during pledge week," Kathleen explained proudly. "She and a lot of the pledges refused to obey their big sisters—and were promptly dismissed from the Greek scene."

"Which is okay by me," Missy assured Miranda. "I don't need some dumb old sorority to make me popular."

"That's for sure. Right now, she's dating the entire swim team," Kathleen joked. "She's going through them one bald head at a time."

Missy frowned. "It's not that bad," she said. "Can I help it if I like athletic guys with big shoulders? Besides I've only dated three guys from the swim team."

"And I'll bet one of them is upstairs right now, shaving the nubs from his chrome dome," Kathleen suggested.

"The team members shave their heads and bodies to pick up speed in the water," Missy explained to Miranda. "Roger left an hour ago." She paused and took a big sip of her iced tea. "Anyhow, I'm busy with math classes. I'm an actuarial science major. I've got a huge workload."

Miranda wasn't sure what actuarial science was, but it sounded impressive.

"I live with a genius!" Kathleen said, smiling. "I'm out of my league."

"Don't you believe her," Missy assured Miranda. "Kat here's a top-notch communications major. Her professor said that her last project was the best he'd ever seen."

"We had to come up with a premise for a reality show," Kathleen spoke up proudly. "I called mine *Surviving Love and Home Improvement*. "It's sort of like a mix of *Survivor*, *The Bachelor*, and *Trading Spaces*. There's this one single guy and twelve women all stranded on an island, and they have to take turns decorating his hut by using only things that they find around them. Then he picks one girl to be his fiancée."

"That sounds bizarre," Miranda said. Then she blushed. The words had popped out before she could stop them.

But Kathleen wasn't insulted. In fact, she sort of agreed. "Bizarre is what people want. And you know guys will go for anything that has a girl in a bikini wearing a tool belt. It's one of their strange fantasies."

Miranda giggled as she sat back in the beanbag and took a big gulp of the iced tea. Already she was beginning to feel better. The room seemed more cheerful as she allowed the air conditioning to take the heat from her body, and these girls seemed genuinely nice—if a little unlike anyone she'd ever known.

Of course, there would be a lot of people like that in her life now. This wasn't Barton, after all. In Barton, everyone was pretty much the same: some richer, some poorer, but basically all cut from the same cloth. It wasn't going to be like that in Austin. But wasn't that part of the reason she'd gone for a city college? So she could meet other kinds of people?

"So what do you think, Miranda?"

Kathleen asked her. "Do you want to see the third bedroom?"

"Sure," Miranda agreed. "Just lead the way."

By Thursday evening, Miranda finally felt settled in at the house. Her things were folded and put away in the milk crates Kathleen had helped her find behind the all-night market near the house, and she'd managed to find a few posters to hang on the wall. She'd gone to the student center to get her precalculus book, and actually seemed to be understanding the stuff in the first chapter.

Miranda was getting used to life in Austin—or at least parts of it. There were still some odd things she wasn't sure she'd ever get used to, like the sound of traffic driving past her window in the middle of the night; the all-night diner down the block with the neon light that blinked on and off and sent bright orange and blue light streaming through her room at all hours; or, most of all, the irony that, despite all the thousands of people in the city, she'd never been more alone in her life.

Back in high school, she'd never eaten one meal alone. There was always someone in the cafeteria to sit with, no matter what period she'd had lunch. And when she was hungry after school, she could always head over to Jilly's Burgers, in the center of town, where chances were a crowd of teenagers were already hanging out there.

But she didn't know anyone in Austin. And for the first time, Miranda had become one of those people she and Cally had always felt sorry for: the ones who brought a book to the diner so they had something to do while they ate alone.

Not that her roommates deliberately excluded her whenever they could. It was just that they had their own interests.

Missy's idea of evening entertainment was of a more *personal* nature. Her boyfriend "du jour" (as Kathleen liked to put it), Roger, was cute if you like the muscle-bound, bald-headed type—sort of like Vin Diesel with a Southern accent. He was spending the summer in Austin, retaking his Introduction to Composition class. Missy was supposedly helping him write his essays for the class. Miranda had a feeling that there wasn't a whole lot of typing going on there.

Kathleen spent most of her time hanging out with her boyfriend, Jay, a guitarist with a local garage band. Between her time with Jay and her job at the housing office, the tall brunette was hardly ever around.

So Miranda spent a lot of time studying by herself. At the moment, she was so involved in making sense of her precalc assignment and listening to her Dixie Chicks CD on her Walkman that she didn't notice Kathleen had entered the room until the girl was right in her face. Miranda looked up into Kathleen's heavily eyelinered eyes and smiled. "Hi," she greeted her as she took off her headphones. "What's up?"

"I'm off to Jay's rehearsal," Kathleen replied. "You're sure you don't want to come with me tonight?"

Miranda hadn't met Jay yet, but she had seen his picture on Kathleen's bureau. In the photo the two of them looked like they were headed for some sort of punk funeral: she in her black leather pants and funky black lace-up bustier, and he with his mohawk, black boots, black jeans, and vintage Ramones T-shirt (black, of course). Miranda figured Jay couldn't possibly play in a band that performed the kind of music she'd be interested in.

"No thanks," Miranda answered with a smile. "I've got a hot date tonight with my math book. Quiz tomorrow."

"Already?" Kathleen sounded suprised. "Class just started Tuesday."

Miranda shrugged. "The professor said we had to work twice as hard because we're doing a whole semester's worth of work in six weeks."

"He wasn't kidding," Kathleen agreed. "Anyway, maybe you'll come next week. We have a good time. Usually after rehearsal, the guys in the band like to go hang out at one of the clubs on Red River Street. There's always a few good bands jamming on a Thursday night."

"Sure," Miranda agreed. "Maybe next time."

"Okay, then. See ya later." Kathleen turned and headed out of the room. "Ciao for now."

As the front door slammed shut, Miranda leaned back and tried to focus on her math. *Bam. Bam. Bam.* Suddenly, there was a terrible banging coming from the other side of the wall. The noise startled her. Something terrible was happening in Missy's room. It was that Roger. He was so strong. Maybe they'd had a fight. Maybe he was hurting her.

Instantly, Miranda leaped up and grabbed the nearest heavy object she could find, which just happened to be her calculus book. "Don't worry, Missy. I'm coming!" she shouted at the top of her lungs as she leaped into the hallway and raced to Missy's door. But before she could even turn the knob, she heard voices coming from the room.

"Oh, yeah!" Missy cried out.

Miranda blushed and leaped back from the door as though it were on fire. Missy didn't need her help at all. She and Roger were obviously just . . . what was it Denny liked to call it when people got crazy-wild like that? . . . Oh yeah: "Bucking the bronco."

Denny.

Just the thought of him made Miranda homesick. It was Thursday evening. If she were home right now they'd probably be going for a sunset horseback ride toward the lake behind his house. She'd be on his sister's palomino, Sparkle, and he'd be riding Chester, his large brown stallion. That was what summer evenings were about in Barton. Long, lazy rides, watching the sun set, and hanging out with the people who knew you best.

Miranda had to wonder what Denny was doing now. Was he alone in his room, too, thinking about her? Somehow, Miranda doubted it. Denny wasn't exactly a big thinker. No. He was probably out partying with some friends, maybe drinking Jack Daniel's in the stables near Carson's house, or swimming in Cally's pool. Unless . . . Miranda shut her eyes, trying to block out the thought. But she couldn't. It nagged at her like a fly buzzing around a horse's eye. What if Denny was riding Chester down to the lake right now? And what if someone else was riding Sparkle beside him?

She couldn't think about that now.

There wasn't anything she could do about it anyway. It had been her decision to leave.

Miranda walked slowly back to her room and threw the calculus book on the bed. Then she headed downstairs, flopped down on the couch, and flipped on the TV. She sighed and looked up at the mannequin in the corner of the room. Tonight she was dressed in a leopard-print miniskirt, a purple sweater, and a silver boa. "Well, Mother," Miranda told the mannequin ruefully, "I guess it's just you and me tonight."

Three

By Friday afternoon, things started to seem a little brighter to Miranda. Two of the girls in her precalc class asked her if she wanted to grab dinner with them at a local bar, and Miranda practically leaped at the chance. True, the two girls, Erika and Adrianna, weren't the type of people Miranda would usually hang out with—they were extremely trendy, with their brightly colored miniskirts and white half tank tops, and their copies of *Cosmopolitan* tucked into the front pockets of their backpacks—but at least they were human company. Mother was a little short on conversational skills.

Erika and Adrianna, on the other hand, seemed to have plenty to say. "So where are you from, exactly?" Erika asked Miranda.

"Barton, Texas," Miranda replied. "It's about three and a half hours from here."

"Barton," Erika repeated. "It sounds cute. Like something out of an old movie."

Miranda frowned. Her town was just as modern as any other place. Maybe not as sophisticated as Austin, but few places in the world were. Besides, Miranda had a feeling neither Erika nor Miranda were from big cities either. "Where are you guys from?" she asked, as if to prove it.

"I'm originally from New York City," Adrianna replied.

Okay, so much for instinctive feelings.

"I was brought up just outside Dallas. I'm Texas born and bred."

"Like me," Miranda suggested. But the look on Erika's face made it plain that the girl didn't consider Barton anything like where she was from.

Miranda didn't try to make much conversation after that. Instead, she looked around the dark, wooden restaurant. A broad smile formed on her lips. "Oh, a pool table!" she exclaimed. "Do you guys play?"

Erika and Adrianna looked at her, surprised.

Guess not. "Well, do you mind if I go over and call winners?" Miranda asked. "I *love* pool. I've had a hankering to play."

"A *hankering,* huh?" Erika laughed.

"Go ahead," Adrianna added, waving her hand dismissively.

Miranda walked toward the table, reaching into her pocket and pulling out two quarters. She placed them on the corner of the pool table, indicating that she wanted in on the next game. One of the current players, a tall, dark-haired guy in a gray Molson T-shirt, jeans, and a worn-in pair of cowboy boots looked up from the pool table and smiled at her. "I should probably warn you that I'm about to put this boy out of his misery, and then you'll be up against *me,*" he told her.

Miranda looked over at his opponent. He did look rather miserable. But that didn't scare her. "I think we'll be fairly well matched," she replied. "In fact"—she reached into her pocket and pulled out a five-dollar bill—"I'm willing to bet on it."

"Okay, it's your hide," the tall, dark, sexy pool player replied, sending his last ball into the side pocket and ending the game. He looked Miranda up and down. "It's an awful pretty hide, though. I'd hate to hurt it."

Miranda stared him straight in the eye. "Nice try," she told him. "But I'm not easily psyched out."

Her opponent smiled and stuck out his hand. "Travis," he said.

"Miranda," she replied, shaking his hand.

"You want to break, Miranda?" he asked, as he racked up the balls.

"Sure, why not?" She picked up a cue and sent the white ball flying into the colorful pyramid of billiard balls. It was a nice break, and the kids who'd gathered around the table seemed impressed.

Miranda and Travis were well matched. But Travis didn't seem at all threatened by being up against such a talented girl. In fact, he sort of seemed to be getting off on it. He smiled at her; even winked a few times. Miranda didn't mind. It was the sort of harmless flirting folks did around a pool table, just like she and her friends would do back home in Barton.

"Nice game," Travis congratulated her. "But I'm afraid you've met your match." He reached over, aimed his cue, and expertly finished off the game.

Miranda watched as the ball went into the pocket, and frowned. She wasn't sad at losing so much as she was upset that her fun had ended. Now she'd have to go back to Erika and Adrianna. What a letdown *that* would be.

Miranda handed her five dollars to Travis. "Here you go, champ."

Travis smiled and shook his head. "Nah. It's okay."

"You won it fair and square."

"Yeah, I did," he agreed. "But I can't take money from a lady. However . . ." He paused for a minute, looking her over with an appreciating eye. "I could take a *beer* from a lady. How about buying me a brew? We can sit over there and hang out for a while."

"Aren't you going to slaughter your next victim?" Miranda asked, indicating the short-haired computer geek who'd stepped up to the table.

"Oh, that would just be cruel," Travis said. They shared a laugh at the poor guy's expense. "Come on. Let's have that beer."

Miranda headed over to the bar and got two beers. She brought the mugs back to the table and took a seat, taking note that Travis had pulled her chair onto the same side of the table as his.

Travis grinned and took a big gulp of his beer. "So where'd you learn to play pool like that?"

"My boyfriend . . . I mean . . ." Miranda stopped herself. Denny wasn't really her boyfriend anymore, was he? "My *ex*-boyfriend has a pool table in his game room. We played there all the time."

"I'll bet you did," Travis said, eyeing her in a way that made her feel slightly uncomfortable. "Where are you from?"

"A small town. You've probably never heard of it. "

"I'm from one of those," Travis told her.

Miranda was just about to say something when Travis leaned over and placed his mouth against hers. He plunged his tongue deep into her mouth.

"Hey! What do you think you're

doing?" Miranda exclaimed, jumping away.

"Come on, honey," he said in his slow, Texas drawl. "You know you want it. We're on the same wavelength."

"We are not!"

"Don't go all hard-to-get on me now, baby. You've been flirting with me ever since you walked over to the pool table."

Miranda blushed wildly.

"Hey, it's cool," he continued. "I was flirting with you too. Besides, what's wrong with a little animal magnetism? Like the bulls and cows in your daddy's barn."

Miranda was fuming now. "My daddy doesn't have a barn. But you're right about one thing: You *are* acting like an animal!"

"I like it when a girl gets feisty," Travis admitted.

"Then you'll love this!" She reached back, made a fist, and knocked him straight in the eye. His chair fell backward, making a loud crash. "Is that wild enough for you?" she demanded.

It was only after she'd turned and stormed toward the door that Miranda noticed the restaurant had grown silent. Everyone was staring at her.

"Can you believe her?" Adrianna murmured as Miranda passed. "What does she think this is—the O.K. Corral?"

"That country bumpkin is definitely not our kind," Erika agreed.

The words stung in Miranda's ears hours later as she sat alone in her room, staring at the peeling paint and feeling hideously alone. She was so embarrassed. Miranda wasn't usually the type to cause a scene. But Travis had crossed the line, and she'd instinctively lashed out. She'd tried calling Cally so she could cry on a friendly shoulder, but her best pal wasn't picking up her cell. As for her roommates, Missy was in her room with the door locked . . . again. And Kathleen was out. Probably staying at her boyfriend's place or something, Miranda figured.

There was nothing to do but study. That was, after all, what she'd come to college for, wasn't it? To get an education. She hadn't come here to make friends or be popular. She would just bury herself in her work. That's all. The summer would go faster that way. Hell, maybe if she worked real hard she could get out of school in three years instead of four.

It wasn't a particularly comforting thought.

An hour or so later, Miranda's head was buried in her book when there was a knock at her door. "Yes?"

"It's Kathleen. I saw the light on in your room."

"Come on in," Miranda said, putting down her book and sitting up tall on her bed. "It's open."

"Studying on a Friday night?" Kathleen asked as she entered the room. "Girl, you need a life."

That's the understatement of the year. "I was out before, but . . ." No sooner were the words out of her mouth than the tears began to fall. Harsh, bitter tears, which seemed to burn the skin off her face. The story of the horrible night then poured out of her, every heinous detail— from start to finish. Kathleen listened to all of it, passing no judgment, until

Miranda got to the part about decking Travis.

"All right, Miranda! The women of Texas should bow down and kiss your feet."

"That's not how Erika and Adrianna saw it," Miranda replied ruefully.

"Oh, and you're going to take the bimbo brigade seriously?" Kathleen asked.

"You know them?" Miranda asked, surprised.

"Well, maybe not those two personally, but I know their type. What were you doing with them, anyhow?"

Miranda shrugged. "They asked me to go to dinner. It didn't seem like it would be a bad idea. But I shouldn't have gone. I knew right away we weren't going to have a good time. I didn't fit in with them."

"You should be proud of that. You should also be proud of the fact that you stuck them with the check."

Miranda groaned. "Ooh, I forgot all about that. I'll give them the money on Monday."

"Why?" Kathleen asked. "Consider it an entertainment fee. After all, it sounds like you gave 'em quite a show."

Miranda blushed. "That's so not like me. I don't fight people. You should have known me back home. I'm really mellow. I just like to hang out with my crowd and . . . well, the thing is, I don't have any crowd here. I don't really fit in with anyone." She sighed.

"That's not so," Kathleen replied, sounding very indignant. "You fit in with *us*. For starters, I know Mother thinks the world of you."

Miranda frowned. "Very funny."

"No, seriously. You and I aren't so different."

Miranda looked at Kathleen, with her dark black eyeliner, vintage Sex Pistols T-shirt, and varied piercings. What could she and this girl possibly have in common?

"We both came here knowing no one, trying to forge our own paths," Kathleen explained. "I picked one that's a whole hell of a lot different from who I was at home, and you probably will too. But you're never going to change until you break away from all those beliefs your parents and friends have crammed down your throat all these years."

"I'm not so sure I *want* to change."

Kathleen gave her a knowing look. "Okay, maybe not change, but *grow.* And you do want to do that. Otherwise, you would've stayed home and married that guy you told us about—what was his name? Donny?"

"Denny."

"Right. Denny. You would have married him and lived your little housewife life in your old hometown. But you came here. Obviously there was some part of you that didn't want to be stuck in a small-town rut. You came to Austin. That was your first step toward breaking free. Now you've got to try hard to completely break out of the mold. Do something a little crazy. Something completely out of character."

"I don't know what you mean."

Kathleen sighed. "There must be something you've always wanted to do or try that you just couldn't see yourself doing back in Boonton."

"Barton."

"*Wherever,*" Kathleen said, and sighed. "The point is, you won't find out who you are unless you look for the one thing that makes you special, different. It's in there somewhere, buried under eighteen years of sweet, down-home conditioning."

"I guess . . . ," Miranda mused, sounding unsure.

"Well, at least think about it, okay?"

Miranda nodded.

"And in the meantime, why don't you and I go down to the kitchen? I think I spotted a whole container of Chunky Monkey in the freezer."

"Okay," Miranda agreed. "And while we're at it, we can go really crazy and pour chocolate sauce all over it."

Kathleen chuckled. "Now you're getting in the spirit of things."

Four

The house was really quiet when Miranda awoke on Saturday morning. Rather than sit around by herself—again—she decided to get moving and explore the ultracool neighborhood she'd seen the first day she'd arrived.

As she hopped off the bus in the West End, Miranda spotted a local Starbucks and quickly ran in for a large Frappuccino to go.

Mmm . . . a sip from home. That was the nice thing about chains like Starbucks, Burger King, and the Gap. They all looked the same, no matter which one you went to. They were like familiar neighbors that traveled with you wherever you went.

Of course, familiarity, and same-old—same-old were the exact root of her troubles, at least according to Kathleen. Miranda guessed she probably should have at least stopped in the little café on the corner for an ice coffee. At least it would have been a little bit different.

She glanced at the store window in front of her. The clothes were definitely not her usual style. The mannequins were all clothed in tight, brightly colored skirts, belly shirts, and jeweled high-heel shoes. For a moment Miranda considered going inside and trying something on, but then she thought better of it. Those clothes would look a whole lot better on Mother than they ever would on her.

And then something caught her eye that struck her as a perfect fit. A little sign, stapled to a post on the sidewalk, it read:

DISCOVER THE BEAT
OF YOUR OWN DRUMMER.
Learn to drum from one of Austin's top percussion teachers. All levels welcome.

Then it listed a phone number and an

address. Miranda didn't know why the sign had gotten her attention; it was just a small, plain sheet of paper. But now that she'd focused on it, she couldn't seem to turn away. *Drum lessons.* That sounded kind of cool. Very un-Miranda. Which was exactly what the doctor—or, in this case, *Kathleen*—had ordered.

Of course, she'd never thought of herself as particularly musical—or rhythmical. She chuckled to herself, remembering the time her daddy had tried to teach her the Texas two-step before a father-daughter dance at the middle school. She just couldn't stick with the beat, and wound up stepping on her dad's feet more than the floor. *Drumming— yeah, right. What was she thinking?*

Still, she checked the map she'd been carrying in her purse, and tried to locate the address. Hmm . . . it wasn't far, just a block or two. She could find it easily. The fact that the drum studio was so close and easily accessible struck Miranda as some sort of sign. She turned and headed off toward the studio. It couldn't hurt to just get some information, anyway.

The address on the sheet led Miranda to a small music shop on a nearby side street. It seemed small for a place where they gave drum lessons. At least from what Miranda could tell, the store was filled with music books and instruments for sale. She walked up to the counter and approached a heavy-set man with a shaved head. He was wearing a short-sleeve shirt and khaki shorts. He had a large tattoo on his forearm, and wore several thick silver rings, one of which looked like a skeleton's head. "Excuse me," she said shyly. "I, um . . . came to ask you about the drum lessons. I saw the sign on a pole on Sixth Street and—"

The balding guy nodded. "Oh, you want *Paul,*" he said. He turned toward a stairwell just behind the counter. "Paul," he shouted downstairs, "some girl's here about your ad."

Miranda breathed a sigh of relief. So this fellow wasn't the drum teacher after all. Well, that was a good thing. She couldn't see herself spending any time alone in a studio with someone who looked so menacing.

But she could see herself spending time with

us. . . . Miranda's eyes burst open wide, and her heart pounded slightly as quite possibly the most gorgeous specimen of masculinity she'd ever seen emerged from the stairwell. He looked about twenty or twenty-one, and he was tall and muscular, with large green eyes and blondish short hair. His face was perfectly oval shaped, and he had just the hint of a cleft in his chin.

"Hi. I'm Paul."

Miranda blushed, realizing suddenly that she had been staring—no, make that *gaping*—at the man in a pretty obvious fashion. She stuck out her hand quickly. "I'm Miranda. I . . . um . . . well . . . I saw your sign on the post, and drumming sounded cool, even though I'm not really very musical, and . . ." *Ah, jeez. Could she sound any more stupid?*

But Paul didn't seem to think she sounded idiotic. In fact, he smiled again. "It *is* pretty cool. And I'll bet you're more musical than you think. Most people are."

Miranda shrugged. "I don't know about that."

"Only one way to find out," Paul

replied, pointing his hand in the direction of the stairwell. "I have a small kit set up downstairs. Why not give it a try now?"

Now? "Well, I . . . I mean . . . the thing is . . ." *There she went again, sounding like a complete idiot.*

"Come on," Paul urged.

The idea of going downstairs with this guy definitely didn't sound too unpleasant. But there *was* one problem. "I don't have a lot of money with me," Miranda told him.

"That's okay," he assured her. "The first lesson's a free trial."

"It is?" said the big guy behind the counter, sounding surprised. "Since when?"

"Since this charming person walked into the shop, Jerry," Paul told him. "Come on, Miranda. What have you got to lose?"

"Nothing, I guess," she replied as she turned and followed Paul down into the studio.

"Now hold the sticks this way," Paul said, adjusting Miranda's fingers slightly so that she was gripping the wooden drumsticks properly.

She sat there for a minute, feeling the

warmth of his body so close to hers. It made it hard to concentrate on the instructions he was giving her. For a moment, she felt strangely disloyal to Denny, which was ridiculous, she knew. After all, it wasn't like Paul was showing any interest in her other than as a potential student. And, more importantly, she hadn't heard from Denny in almost a month. He'd obviously broken up with her—at least in his mind, if not officially.

"Okay, now tap here with your left hand," Paul said, moving her hand up and down over one of the drums to show her how the motion would feel. "And at the same time, move your right hand, here."

Miranda tried to do as he told her, but it was tough. Her hands seemed to want to move at exactly the same time, but that wasn't what they were supposed to do.

"No, try *alternating* the beats," Paul told her patiently. "Follow my lead. Left, right, left, right . . . that's it. You've got it now."

Much to Miranda's surprise, she really *did* have the beat down. Paul moved slightly away from her and flicked the knob on a nearby stereo. A song began to play—some seventies oldies thing that Miranda vaguely remembered hearing her dad sing along to in the truck once in a while. Suddenly she realized she was playing along with it. *And she didn't sound half bad.*

"Wow! You're a natural," Paul complimented her.

He probably said that to all his potential students, but Miranda didn't care. It *did* feel incredibly natural. She liked being surrounded by all of the drums and cymbals. It was like the drum set was her own little domain. And the sticks didn't feel quite so awkward now that she'd gotten the rhythm and motion down. A smile began to form on her lips. As the song ended, she reached up and gave the cymbal a hard slam—just like she imagined a real rock star might.

"Okay, *that* was a little over the top." Paul laughed, putting his hands up to his ears playfully. "But you have the idea."

"That was so much fun!" Miranda exclaimed. "Can we try it with a different song?"

"Actually, I have a lesson in a few minutes," Paul told her. "But we can schedule something for later in the week."

"Oh," Miranda replied, disappointed. "Okay. Um . . . but . . . how much does a regular lesson cost?"

"My usual fee is thirty-five dollars a half hour, but we can negotiate if . . ."

Miranda did somes quick mental calculations. Her rent at the house was less than the dorms would have cost her, so that gave her a few extra dollars. And if she packed her lunch instead of eating at the burger joint in the Student Activities Center, she could spare thirty-five dollars a week. "It's okay. I could do that," she told him quickly.

"All right!" Paul sounded genuinely excited. "When you go upstairs, just work out a time with Jerry."

Miranda reluctantly handed him back the drumsticks. "I guess I'll have to wait till next week to play again," she said. "I can't afford to buy a drum set just yet."

Paul thought for a moment. "I have an old pad kit in the back you can borrow to practice on if you want."

"A *pad* kit?"

"Yeah. They're not actually drums, just

these soft pads on stands that you can set up to resemble a drum kit. The bounce on the pads simulates the way a real kit would feel while you were playing. But they don't actually make any noise—which is something I'll bet your roommates'll be grateful for."

Miranda smiled. Considering the amount of banging she heard coming from Missy's room, she doubted they'd care. "That would be great," she thanked him.

"Wait here. I'll get it for you," Paul said as he put down the sticks and turned, heading down a narrow hallway.

As soon as he left the room, Miranda leaped up and grabbed the sticks like a naughty impulsive child secretly sticking her fingers in the cookie jar. Then she began banging out the rhythm on the drums. She couldn't help herself. It was just so much fun. But the minute Paul entered the room, she stopped, embarrassed at being caught. Not that he couldn't have heard her down the hall. It must've sounded pretty awful to a professional like him.

Surprisingly, Paul seemed genuinely impressed with her attempts at playing.

"That's pretty good," he complimented her as he entered the room. "You're getting it." He stood the pad kit up and motioned for her to come closer and watch what he was doing. "All you need to do is unfold the metal stands. Then set the pads up the same way these drums are set up."

With several swift, confident motions, he opened the kit and set it up to show her. Miranda watched intensely, consciously trying to focus on the task at hand rather than on the way his muscles bulged beneath his short-sleeve T-shirt as he worked.

"Okay, I think I can do that," Miranda said.

"Great. And I also brought you a pair of sticks. They're my old ones, but I think they have a little life left in them."

Miranda took the sticks in her hands. She suddenly felt a huge wave of gratitude, as though this perfect stranger had given her some sort of amazing gift; something much more valuable than just two old drumsticks. The gaze that was returned to her through Paul's eyes assured her that he knew exactly how she felt. It was a weird moment of intimacy between two perfect strangers, yet neither of them seemed the least bit uncomfortable.

"Paul, your noon lesson's here," Jerry called down suddenly.

The mood was broken. "That's my cue," Paul told her, moving his eyes from hers.

"Okay, see you next week," Miranda replied, taking the sticks and the pad kit and heading toward the stairs.

Five

"Miranda, you're doing it again," Kathleen reminded her. The girls were seated at the breakfast table, munching on eggs and toast.

"Oops, sorry," Miranda said, putting down her knife and fork. "I swear, I don't even realize it anymore."

"Trust me, you're drumming. In fact, you drum on everything."

Miranda nodded. It had been just a few weeks since she'd started taking lessons with Paul, and already it had become an obsession. "I know. My math professor brought it up to me twice yesterday. I was drumming on the table with my pencil while I worked on my midterm. He said I was going to have to take the test in the hall if I didn't stop. It was so embarrassing. I felt like I was back in elementary school."

"Well, you have to look at it from his point of view," Missy reminded her. "The other students were probably having trouble concentrating while listening to your para . . . para . . . what do you call those things again?"

"Paradiddles," Miranda replied. "And I know you're right. I felt terrible."

"You've got to find another place to drum," Missy continued. "I hear the pads right through my wall. They're not *completely* silent."

Now *that* made Miranda angry. It wasn't like Missy didn't make her own share of noise. Maybe Missy needed to find another place to practice *her* hobby too.

Of course, Miranda would never say that. She wasn't the type to complain. And she couldn't really, anyway. She'd only been in the house a few weeks. She was the newcomer. She didn't want to be the troublemaker too. After all, these girls had been really nice to her. They'd taken her in and made her feel a part of things when she had nowhere else to go.

She turned toward Kathleen. Surely *she* would understand. After all, her boyfriend was a musician. If anyone would know how important it was to be able to play . . .

But Kathleen wasn't nearly as sympathetic as Miranda might have hoped. "We're glad you love the drums," she began. "But the thing is, you're kind of making us nuts."

Miranda frowned. Well, that was that. Without Kathleen on her side, there was no way she was going to be able to keep on using her pad kit in the house. If she couldn't practice, she would never improve. And she really did want to work on her chops—as Paul called it. Miranda sighed. Her roommates were wrong: Drumming wasn't a hobby, it was a *passion*. She felt free and wild behind the drums. For a girl who was usually much more quiet and reserved, the emotion was irresistable.

And now she was going to have to give it all up. A physical pain raced through her body, and she thought she might throw up.

"I, um . . . I have to go," she said, getting up from the table and quickly throwing her uneaten eggs in the trash.

Miranda was in tears as she arrived at the studio, the old pad kit in hand. Jerry looked up from the desk, surprised. "Miranda," he greeted her. "Do you have a lesson today?" He glanced at the pile of papers in front of him. "I don't think you're on the sheet."

"I . . . I . . ." Miranda shook her head, unable to say the words. "I have to give this to Paul. Is he here?"

As if on cue, Paul emerged from downstairs. "Did I hear my name?" he asked. Then he noticed Miranda standing there, the pad kit in hand. "Oh, hey Rand. What's up?"

"My roommates . . . they . . ."

"Oh . . . the *roommates*," Paul said knowingly. He wrapped a strong arm around Miranda and pulled her tight. "The drummers' dilemma."

"They say I can't practice in the house anymore. I'm driving everyone crazy, and . . ."

"Let me guess—the walls are shaking, the vibrations are keeping them awake, and your constant drumming on things is a pain."

Miranda nodded and wiped the tears from her cheek.

"Welcome to the world of percussion. People just have no tolerance. Sometimes I think we drummers should all go and live on an island somewhere. Then we can bang on *anything* we want *whenever* we want."

"Your neighbors would second that idea," Jerry said, laughing, trying to break the tension. "Hell, they'd even pack your bags."

But neither Miranda nor Paul noted the humor. To them this was a serious issue. "It's not like I'm doing it on purpose," Miranda explained. "It just sort of happens. Most of the time I don't even realize I'm drumming."

"I know," Paul assured her. "It's as though your fingers have a mind of their own."

Miranda sighed. That was it exactly. "They want me to practice somewhere else. But I don't have the money to rent a space, and the rehearsal rooms at Lone Star State are only for matriculated music majors. I can't even audition for that until I can play better. I mean, it's only been a few weeks. And now, even if I wanted to try out for the School of Music, I can't, because I have to give up drumming and—"

"Whoa, hold on," Paul said, stopping her. "Who says you have to give up the drums?"

"Haven't you been listening?" Miranda asked him. "I have no place to practice."

"Well, why not practice here?"

"Because I don't have any money. I'm living on mac and cheese as it is to pay for the lessons. I can't afford studio space too."

Paul looked at Jerry. "Weren't you looking for someone to help out part-time with the paperwork?" he asked him.

Jerry nodded. "I can't keep track of the lesson book, and order forms for sheet music and deal with the billing at the same time."

"Well, what if we make a deal with Miranda here? She works three afternoons a week, and we let her use the studio space after hours."

Miranda's eyes grew wide. "You mean like a barter system?"

"Exactly," Paul said. "We have something you need, and you can give us what we need." He turned to Jerry. "What do you say, Jer?"

"I like the idea of not having to pay her cash," Jerry agreed.

"It's not like anyone's using the space in the evenings, anyway," Paul reminded him. "Things are kind of slow in the summer— till the fresh crop of college kids file in in September." He chuckled slightly at some joke he and Jerry shared.

"I guess it's fine with me, then," Jerry agreed. But he didn't chuckle back. In fact, he frowned just a bit.

"Oh, Paul! You're the greatest!" Miranda shouted. She leaped up in the air and wrapped her arms around his broad shoulders. Paul laughed and hugged her tightly.

Jerry sighed. "Why is it always the good-looking guys who get the hugs?"

Miranda giggled and then went over to give Jerry a peck on the cheek. The big guy blushed like a schoolboy. Then he reached over and handed her a folder with a stack of loose papers. "These are all the scheduled lessons. See if you can get them in some sort of order, will ya?" he told her, trying to sound gruff but not quite able to.

Later that night, after all the lessons were over, Miranda went downstairs into the basement studio. She sat down behind the drumset and started to hit the skins. It was amazing being able to play real drums with no one around. She could hear as well as feel the beat, and she didn't have to feel as though she were being judged by her teacher. It was just herself and the drums, and it was a feeling she'd never experienced.

Miranda had no idea how long she'd been playing, when she suddenly became aware that someone else had entered the studio. She looked up and stopped immediately, blushing with embarrassment at the thought of someone hearing and watching her—especially since that someone was Paul. "I . . . uh . . . I was just . . . ," she murmured, blushing.

"You were amazing," he told her with a

knowing grin. "You're a natural. You were able to take what you've learned and put your own spin on it. That's what artists do."

Artists. Miranda had never thought of herself as an artist. That was more Cally's role, in their crowd back home. Cally was the one with all the talent, what with the screenplays she wrote, and the photography and videos she was always so focused on.

But Miranda wasn't back home anymore. She was in Austin. And this man—*a professional drummer*—had called her an artist. It was hard to believe.

"Here, let me show you a better way to approach the high hat so the sound doesn't become overbearing," Paul said, moving behind her and wrapping his arms around hers to help her move her wrists.

Miranda gasped slightly. Almost instantly, she found herself losing track of the rhythm Paul was trying to show her, focusing instead on the beating of his heart. She tensed slightly, trying to regain her concentration, hoping he hadn't noticed her momentary lapse.

But, of course, he had. "You're off the

beat," he whispered. The gentle breathing in her ear tickled slightly, and a shiver of excitement ran through her.

Paul sensed her emotions and immediately dropped his arms from around her. But instead of pulling back from the situation, he moved closer and, with one fluid motion, turned her slightly so the seat of her chair swiveled in his direction. He took her hand in his, pulled her to her feet, and kissed her hard.

Miranda jumped back for a moment, surprised at the intensity of his kiss. But she wasn't upset or frightened. In fact, she was excited, and glad that Paul had made the first move. She'd never have had the guts to have done that. But now that he'd taken the lead . . .

Miranda looked up into his green eyes and then melted into his arms as she felt his warm lips pressing against hers once more.

Six

"Miranda, your eyes are going to pop out of your head if you keep staring at the door that way," Missy teased. It was eleven o'clock, Thursday night. The girls' house was in full-party mode. Miranda had invited Paul and Jerry to this midsummer blast, but as of yet, they still hadn't shown up.

"They're not coming," Miranda predicted, sighing. "Paul didn't want to come to a college party, but I thought Jerry had finally persuaded him. I guess I was wrong."

"They'll be here," Missy assured her. She handed her a small paper cup filled with bright yellow gelatin. "Want a shot?"

"Of Jell-O?"

"This is Kathleen's *special* Jell-O. It's made with vodka."

Miranda took the cup of yellow Jell-O and nibbled a bit from the top. It tasted weird—sort of a mix of bitter and sweet all at once. She made a face. "You like these?"

Missy shrugged. "I'm more the sex-on-the-beach type."

Miranda stared at her in amazement. She'd never met someone so blasé about sex before.

Missy giggled at Miranda's reaction. "That's a drink, silly," she assured her.

Miranda blushed and looked away from Missy. Sure enough, there were plenty of empty paper cups around. And, judging by the wild dancing and laughter going on, the Jell-O shots were already having their desired effect—mostly with Kathleen's friends, though. She could spot them a mile away, in their gloomy black clothing.

At the moment, though, Kathleen was standing off to the side, talking to someone very unlike the kids in her crowd. This guy was wearing a pair of well-worn jeans and a faded blue T-shirt. His hair was chin length and slightly shaggy. He could have come from Barton, or just about any other small town in Texas. Miranda laughed. Kathleen seemed to have a soft spot for people like that. She collected them, like stray puppies. She'd taken *her* in, after all.

"He's kind of cute, isn't he?" Missy noted interrupting Miranda's thoughts.

"Who?"

"The guy you're staring at. You know, the one over there with Kathleen."

"I wasn't staring," Miranda replied indignantly. But the blush that came to her cheeks revealed she was lying.

"It's okay, I don't think he noticed," Missy assured her. "Adam's kind of clueless about stuff like that. He doesn't even know how hot he is."

"Who is he?"

"Adam Burns. He's the bass player for Sin-Phony."

"Oh, he's a musician," Miranda noted with interest.

"Mm-hmm. You two have a lot in common," Missy agreed with a conspiratory smile. "In fact . . ." She turned suddenly to face Kathleen and her friend. "Hey, Adam," she shouted out.

He looked up and smiled in her direction. "Hi, Missy," he shouted back over the din of the crowd.

"Come here," Missy called to him.

"Oh God, Missy, no," Miranda pleaded. She turned away, mortified. Her face was redder than her roommate's hair. "Please . . ."

But it was too late. He was already standing there.

"Wassup, Missy?" Adam asked.

Miranda smiled at the sound of his voice—deep and strong, with a definite Texas accent. He was obviously a native of the state, just like she was.

"I want you to meet our new roommate, Miranda," Missy told him. "You two have a lot in common. Miranda's a drummer."

"Oh, a fellow musician." Adam gave her a warm smile.

"Well, not exactly, I just started playing a few weeks ago, but . . ."

"Well, I'll leave you two to talk tunes," Missy said, making no pains to hide her attempt at matchmaking as she strolled away.

"She's really something," Adam said, noting Miranda's discomfort at the situation.

"Yeah," Miranda agreed.

"So are you new to Austin?" Adam asked.

Miranda nodded. "I'm taking a summer class at Lone Star College."

"Really? Me too," Adam told her. "A film class."

"Oh, are you a film major?" Miranda asked him.

"I think I'm heading in that direction," Adam said. "I don't have to declare until later this year. I'm thinking I might want to score movies."

"Score?" Miranda asked, unsure of what he meant.

"You know, write the incidental music," Adam said.

Miranda blushed. If he hadn't been sure of her amateur musician status before, he was now. "My best friend Cally's a film major at UCLA," Miranda said, anxious to change the subject from her own ignorance. "She wants to direct."

"Cool," Adam replied.

There wasn't much else to say after that. They just sort of stared at each other for a moment. It was extremely uncomfortable. Then Miranda remembered the tray of Jell-O shots Missy had left on the windowsill beside them. "You want a Jell-O shot?" she asked him.

Adam shook his head. "Nah. I've got an early basketball game tomorrow morning."

"Oh wow, that sounds like fun," Miranda told him. "What position do you play?"

"Point guard," Adam replied. "I'm not tall enough to play center."

Miranda looked at him. He wasn't overly tall, it was true. But he looked to be about six feet or so—which was pretty tall, in her book. And he did have an athletic body—she could tell by the way his shirt bulged slightly in the upper chest every time he moved his arms.

"Do you like basketball?" Adam asked her.

Miranda nodded. "I wasn't on a team or anything, but we have a basketball hoop in my driveway back home. I could shoot hoops for hours with the guys from the neighborhood. And my dad's a huge sports fan. We got a satellite dish just so he could watch games from all around the country."

Adam smiled. "Sounds like fun."

Miranda shrugged. "It wears kind of thin after a while."

"I guess."

"There's not a whole lot to do in my town," Miranda explained. "A satellite TV is all the entertainment you can get."

"Sounds like my hometown. I'm from Parker's Point, a couple of hours outside Houston." He smiled at the blank expression on her face. "You've probably never heard of it. Very few people have. It's the kind of place that, if you blink while you're driving through, you'll miss it."

Missy grinned. "Just like my hometown. On one side of the sign it says, 'Welcome to Barton.' And on the other side it says, 'You are now leaving Barton.'"

They laughed, both recognizing the familiar jokes. It was kind of like a code between small-town Texans.

Adam opened his mouth to say something, but his voice was drowned out by someone shouting from the doorway.

"Hey, Miranda!"

Miranda turned around and spotted Jerry bursting through the door. He was wearing a green army jacket with the sleeves cut off, a pair of extremely well-worn jeans, and steel-tipped motorcycle boots. A bright red bandanna was wrapped over his head. More than a few eyes turned when he entered the room.

"I think that's a friend of yours," Adam told her.

"Oh, yeah," Miranda said, smiling brightly. "Jerry. He owns the music store where I work. You guys should actually meet."

"Maybe some other time," Adam said. "Right now, I think Kathleen is getting ready to start the Duane Out. I'll talk to you later."

"The what?" Miranda asked. But before she could finish her question, Adam was gone.

"Hey, Jerry," Miranda greeted him. "Glad you could come."

"Wouldn't miss it," Jerry told her. He watched as her eyes moved toward the door. "He's parking the van," he assured her.

"Oh . . . I wasn't . . . ," Miranda began.

"Sure you were," Jerry teased. "It's cool. I'm used to it. And look, there's the crown prince now."

As Miranda looked up, her eyes met Paul's. He seemed a bit different somehow. At the shop he had been so secure and in control. But here, his eyes darted back and forth, like a scared animal making sure there were no surprises waiting for him. He smiled slightly when he spotted Miranda talking to Jerry. It was as though he'd seen a light in a storm of people.

"Hey," he greeted her, giving her a small peck on the lips. "Nice-size crowd."

"Yeah. A lot of folks turned out," Miranda agreed. "But I'm sure glad to see y'all. I don't know too many of these people. You want a Jell-O shot?" She was trying hard to sound mature, as though Jell-O shots were part of her regular diet.

"Oh, yeah!" Jerry agreed. He had no desire to sound mature. In fact, the big dude was acting like a little kid who was about to get a lollipop. "Do you have any lime ones? They're my favorite!"

Miranda laughed. She would never get

used to how incongruous Jerry's appearance was to his personality. "I don't know. You can check. I think they're in the kitchen." She pointed toward the back of the house.

Jerry nodded. "I'm on it." He began to make his way through the crowd. "Out of the way. Big guy coming through." Not so amazingly, the waves of surprised college kids parted like the Red Sea at the sight of the giant dude in biker gear making his way through the crowd.

"So this is where you live," Paul said. "I had a place like this once. Back when I was in school."

"Where'd you go to college?"

"One year at University of Texas," Paul told her. "That was enough for me."

"You didn't like college?"

"Nah. Everyone was acting so holier-than-thou intellectual. I didn't feel like taking all those literature and philosophy classes. I just wanted to play the drums. So I dropped out and followed my dream."

"Well, it worked out for you," Miranda told him.

"What's that supposed to mean?"

"Nothing. I just was saying that college isn't for everyone."

Paul opened his mouth to speak, but before he could, the sound of a loud twanging guitar filled the room.

"What's that?" Miranda asked him.

"Duane Eddy. An old-time twang guitarist."

"Oh. I've never heard of him."

"It's not the kind of thing you study in college," Paul told her. "He's more something you learn from other musicians. I'm actually surprised any of *these* people have even heard of him."

Miranda looked at him strangely. He was sounding so odd. So *superior.* She didn't quite know what to make of it.

"DUANE OUT!" someone shouted from the other side of the room.

Before Miranda knew what was happening, a whole crowd of Kathleen's friends were in the middle of the floor, literally slam dancing to the sounds of the old recording of Duane Eddy's twanging guitar. And there, right in the middle of the crowd, was one guy who really stood out. Jerry was the life of the party, banging into one kid after another, sending them flying across the room. Kathleen's buddies kept coming back for more, as though Jerry's jelly belly were a giant trampoline.

"Woohoo!" Jerry shouted wildly. Then he put his arms down on the floor and kicked his legs high in the air, trying to achieve the perfect handstand. But he'd obviously misjudged his gymnastic ability. Boom. He came crashing down on the hardwood floor. Punk rockers scattered as he fell, like little black ants trying to avoid being squashed by an elephant.

But Jerry wasn't the least bit embarrassed. He just leaped to his feet, shimmied his huge belly back and forth, and went back to dancing. The guy was obviously having a great time.

Miranda wished she could say the same for Paul. He looked miserable, completely out of his element.

Suddenly, he grabbed her hand. "You want to show me your room?" he asked, the twinkle suddenly returning to his eyes.

Miranda looked at him, uncertain of how to react. She wasn't sure she should bring him up to her *bed*room. If she were home, that sure as shootin' wouldn't happen. There were no boys allowed in her room in Barton. Her parents had made that rule clear. Still, the only parent here right now was Mother. And someone had already put a blindfold over Mother's eyes, and taped earplugs to the sides of her plaster-of-Paris head. She couldn't see or hear a thing.

"Sure," Miranda said finally, leading him up the stairs. "It's not much of a room, but it's cheap, and there's a roof over my head . . . which only leaks a little when it rains."

Paul followed her into the room and looked around. It was a pretty spare place. White walls, a bed, a stereo, and one tiny dresser that looked like it had been rescued from the garbage—which, in fact, it had.

There were only three posters on the wall. One was a promotional poster from Zildjian cymbals that he'd given her. Another was of John Bonham, the late wild-man drummer from Led Zeppelin, who'd been nicknamed Bonzo. The last was a banner from Lone Star College. Paul seemed to focus on that one the most.

When his eyes finally turned away, he stared at Miranda for a moment. Then he drew her toward him and kissed her with an intensity that was unlike anything they'd shared before. After a few minutes, he pulled her down onto the bed, his lips never leaving hers for a second as he positioned himself partially on top of her.

His hands then began moving, rubbing her shoulders, her sides, and eventually making their way to the front of her shirt. At first, Miranda began to move with the rhythm of his body, lost in some sort of haze as her body began to feel things she hadn't experienced in a long time. This was different from their make-out sessions in the music shop studio. He was more intense now, more focused, as though he had a very definite goal in mind. Paul obviously wanted her very badly.

Things could go a lot further now, if she were ready. But the thing was, she *wasn't* ready. Even in the fog created by the motions of his gently rubbing hands, and the slight rocking of their bodies on the bed, Miranda knew this wasn't the time. She didn't feel that way about him. At least not yet. How could she, if she was still noticing other cuties—like that Adam guy downstairs? "Paul, please, don't . . . ," she murmured, gently pushing him away.

"Miranda, there's so much I can show you. I can teach you. Things you'll *never* learn in college. . . ."

Miranda knew that to be true. He was older, more experienced. It made it so much more flattering that a man like this respected her enough to make her his lover. But still, it wasn't the right time. She hadn't known Paul long enough to be that intimate with him. This was something Miranda only wanted to share with someone she loved. And she didn't love Paul. She liked him—maybe even had a crush on him. But . . . "I . . . I can't," she murmured. She shimmied out from beneath him and sat up. "I'm just not ready. I need to feel that it's right, and I just don't. Not yet."

Paul took a deep breath. "It's okay. I don't want to force anything on you. I just thought . . ." He paused for a minute. "I keep forgetting how young you are."

"I'm not that young," Miranda replied defiantly.

"Yeah, you are," Paul told her. "But I like that about you. Naivete. Sweetness. It's not something you run into every day."

"You're not mad at me, are you?" she asked.

Paul wrapped a long, muscular arm around her shoulders and pulled her close to him again. "Are you kidding? I'm glad you were honest with me."

"Really?"

Paul nodded. "Really. How about we go downstairs and Duane Out a little. We shouldn't let Jerry have all the fun."

Miranda nodded, grateful that Paul was being so great about all of this. He was really a terrific guy. The boys back home wouldn't have been so easygoing about being rebuffed like that. She'd probably still be fighting one of them off right now instead of going downstairs to rejoin the party. Miranda figured he was probably only two or three years older than Denny, but the difference in maturity was immeasurable.

But he wasn't *completely* mature, either. There was proof enough of that in the middle of the dance floor. As soon as they got downstairs, Paul joined right in with the rest of slam-dancing, Duane-loving, head-bangers, slamming himself off of Jerry's jelly belly with the best of 'em.

"Hey, Rand," Jerry greeted Miranda as she walked into the shop on the Monday morning after the party.

"Hey, party animal," she replied with a grin.

"It was a great shindig," Jerry told her. "Those Jell-O shots rocked."

"So I heard," Miranda replied. "There were hangovers all over town the next day."

"Mine was one of them," Jerry replied. He put his hand to his head as he looked down at the schedule book on the counter. "Hey, are you going home for a week or two before the new semester starts? I just need to know for the scheduling and stuff."

Home. Miranda hadn't even thought about it the past few weeks. She'd been so caught up in everything at the shop—Paul, and her drumming—that Barton had all but disappeared from her consciousness. It suddenly occurred to her that she actually didn't want to go home. There was too much happening in Austin.

Besides, she could just imagine the expressions on her parents' faces if she told them not only that was she taking drum lessons and working at a music store, but was also considering becoming a music major when it came time to declare in the middle of sophomore year. The Lockhearts were practical people. They probably hoped Miranda would go into something more steady, in an office or something. But Miranda was pretty sure that wasn't going to be her thing.

"I'm gonna stay here," Miranda told Jerry firmly. "I've got some things to do before the semester starts, and besides, you people would fall to pieces without me."

Jerry laughed. "You're not kidding. It's about time someone thought about computerizing our lesson schedules." He glanced over and shot the computer a dirty look. "I personally can't stand those things. All that crap about gigabytes and cyberspace. To me, SPAM is a lunch meat. But I guess it's time our little music shop here entered the twentieth century."

"Especially since it's the *twenty-first* century," Miranda reminded him, laughing.

"Oh, yeah." Jerry blushed. "I'm getting older by the minute. Not like our Paulie, though," he continued. "I swear, that guy just gets younger and younger." Jerry rubbed his bald head. "He's the only guy I know whose hair actually gets thicker! He's like Dorian Gray. Hard to believe he hit the big quarter century last spring."

Miranda gulped. *Quarter century?* That made him twenty-five! She'd known he was older than she was, but wow! He was a full *seven years* older than she was. A guy *that old* thought she was worth hanging out with . . . *making out* with. Pretty impressive. She couldn't wait to tell Cally. What a step up from Denny. As she moved behind the desk and began inputting information into the computer, Miranda was feeling mighty pleased with herself.

At closing time, Miranda grabbed her sticks and headed straight for the stairs. She was looking forward to getting in some practice time. But Jerry stopped her. "You want to come to Jessup's with us tonight?" he asked her.

Miranda looked over at Paul, who was

standing near the sheet music. "You're going to Jessup's?" she asked him, surprised.

"Yeah, there's a new band I wanted to check out," he replied nonchalantly.

"And I'm the one who got the tickets," Jerry said proudly. He glanced in Paul's direction, obviously pleased that this time *he'd* been the one to score the seats. "I met one of the waitresses, and she gave them to me."

Miranda didn't know what to say. She'd hoped that Paul and she could spend some time together in the studio. But obviously Paul had made other plans.

Which was okay. *Really.* It wasn't like they had a date or anything. It was just that Paul knew she was coming in today, and usually they hung out together in the studio on the evenings she was in the shop. They'd been spending so much time together that she'd sort of hoped . . .

"Look, you guys don't have to come," Jerry told them. "If you had plans or something."

"I don't. But Miranda does. She's got plenty of work to do on that new rhythm I taught her." Paul sounded very authoritative.

"I can do that another time," Miranda insisted.

Paul shook his head. "You'll never get into Jessup's, anyhow. They check IDs pretty heavily. And they'll be gunnin' for someone like you."

"What do you mean 'someone like me'?"

"Someone who's got *'college girl'* written right across her face," Paul answered her. "She'll never get in, Jer."

Jerry frowned. "I guess not," he replied, not sounding quite as certain as Paul.

"Okay, so that's it. We'll hit the club. Miranda will lock up after she practices," Paul said.

Miranda sighed. It was all settled. Though certainly not to her liking.

Seven

The very next day, right after precalc class, Miranda hopped on a bus and headed toward the studio. She wasn't scheduled to work or have a lesson, but she wanted to be down there, anyway. It was always so much more exciting in that part of town. And frankly, the idea of studying math was decidedly unappealing.

She got off the bus a block away from the studio, in order to stop and pick up an iced tea. While she was at it, she picked up an extra milk for Jerry. How ironic that the big guy's favorite drink was a glass of cold milk.

She turned toward a local coffee bar and

headed for the door. But she was stopped by an image in the store window. There, sitting at a small round table, was Paul. And he wasn't alone. He was there with a girl. Well, not a girl exactly. More like a woman in her twenties. She was bleached blonde and dressed in possibly the tightest top Miranda had ever seen. It was designed to highlight her huge breasts . . . which definitely had to be fake. Nobody was born like *that.*

Paul and the woman were obviously close. *Real close.* At the moment, Paul was playfully giving her a spoonful of whipped cream from his latte, and she was licking it off in an extremely suggestive manner.

Miranda stood there for a moment, staring at them. She wanted to turn away—she knew she *should* turn away—but she couldn't. It was like watching a car wreck.

After a few moments of self-inflicted torture, Miranda finally found the strength to turn and run. She went to the only place she knew she'd find a sympathetic ear: the music shop.

Sure enough, Jerry was behind the counter, helping a customer, when Miranda entered. He looked up and smiled. "Just can't stay away, huh?" he teased as he handed the customer a bag and some change. "Sorry, Paul's not here right now."

"I know," Miranda replied. "He's on a coffee break . . . or *something*."

Jerry studied her face and then knowingly wrinkled his brow. "Oh, I guess you ran into him and Amber. He said they were going for a cup of joe."

"Amber, who's Amber?" Miranda demanded.

"An old friend of his. He ran into her at Jessup's last night. They hadn't seen each other in a while. . . ."

"Well, it sure looks like they made up for last time," Miranda declared with a frown.

Jerry shrugged. "Ah, don't worry about it, Rand. She's no competition for you. He doesn't really like her all that much."

"It sure didn't look that way to me."

"He really doesn't," Jerry vowed. "They've known each other for a long time. He's not into her romantically. She's just a . . . 'a friend with benefits.'"

Miranda eyed him suspiciously. "Pardon me?"

"They don't date or anything. They just sort of have this agreement. You know, they get together once in a while to . . . well . . . um . . ."

Miranda sensed his discomfort. "Never mind, Jerry. I get it."

"It's nothing against you, Miranda. Paul really does believe you're talented. And I think he likes you. It's just that he's not into the whole relationship thing." He studied her face. "I guess I should've mentioned that to you. It's just I thought that maybe this time . . . I mean, you're a great girl, Miranda, and he—"

"I wasn't looking for a relationship either," Miranda declared boldly. But deep down, she couldn't tell if that was actually the truth.

"You had to figure you weren't the first Lone Star College girl Paul's been involved with . . . ," Jerry told her.

"I didn't figure anything," Miranda replied, trying to sound all brave and strong, and failing miserably.

"It's just the college thing, Rand. He can't get past it."

"What college thing?"

Jerry sighed. "I guess he told you he got thrown out of UT."

Miranda shook her head. "He told me he dropped out because it wasn't for him."

"Well, that's not exactly the truth. He couldn't keep up with the work. The only classes he ever passed were his music theory courses. I think being around college kids makes him feel kind of inferior. He's always trying to prove he knows more than they do."

Miranda didn't know what to say. She thought back to that night in her room at the party. Paul had said, "I can teach you things you'll never learn in school." At the time, she hadn't thought anything of it. But now it all made sense.

"He's comfortable with someone like Amber," Jerry continued. "She never finished college either. He doesn't have to prove anything with her."

"He just *sleeps* with her," Miranda noted ruefully.

"They're both in it for the same thing. It's no big deal to them."

"It is to me."

Jerry sighed. "It's funny, you know. . . ."

"What is?" Miranda asked.

"Well, here I am, this big, bald guy with tattoos, and everyone assumes I'm the tough one. But it's Paulie who has a heart of stone."

Miranda sighed. At the moment, she wished *she* had a heart of stone. At least then it would be unbreakable. But Miranda's heart was pretty much torn apart now. Not because of Paul—she knew there was no future for them— she'd never planned on it, really. But because she was going to have to give up working and practicing at the music store. And *that* was going to be painful. But she just didn't see that she had much of a choice. She couldn't hang around there now, not knowing what she knew. Like Denny, she wasn't the kind of person to hang around after she'd been totally humiliated.

Suddenly, Miranda saw it all so clearly. Paul had a thing about showing his superiority to college girls. He could make them idolize him . . . worship him. And probably, in the case of a lot of them, *sleep with him.* It was obvious he had all the moves down: wrapping himself around her and whispering in her ear as he taught her—which, looking back on it, was sickeningly inappropriate behavior for a teacher. It was a routine. A pattern. And she'd fallen for it.

Miranda took a deep breath as she glanced around the shop one last time. Then she reached up and wrapped her arms as far as they would go around Jerry's wide middle. "Bye," she whispered to him. "Thanks for everything."

"Are you sure you won't come out with us tonight?" Missy asked Miranda as she slipped on a pair of pink crystal chandelier earrings. "Most of the guys from the swim team are back in town, and Roger's got some awfully cute friends."

"No thanks," Miranda replied.

"Come on. It's been two weeks since you and Paul broke up. . . ."

"There was nothing to break up," Miranda told her firmly.

"Whatever," Missy continued. "Anyway, it's been two weeks. And you know what they say. If you fall off a horse, you have to mount one again—right away."

Miranda giggled slightly at Missy's interesting word choice.

"You know what I mean." Missy smiled. She placed a blue newsboy cap on her head and tilted it slightly to the side. "What do you think?"

Miranda shook her head and wrinkled her nose. "I think it would look better on Mother."

Missy giggled. "That broad has the biggest wardrobe in the house. Did you see what she's wearing today? I mean, where would a mannequin get her plaster hands on a Juicy T-shirt?"

"Beats me. I was thinking of giving her one of my old tank tops—maybe the black one I spilled bleach on."

"Nah. Mother wouldn't look good in that," Missy replied. "Whenever she wears tank tops you can see the joints where her arms meet her shoulders. That's *extremely* unattractive." She stopped for a minute and frowned. "Nice try."

"What?"

"You were trying to get me off the topic. I was saying how you should come out with me and the team tonight. You'd have fun. Besides, you deserve it. You need to celebrate that B plus you got in precalc. Not to mention the fact that you've decided not to move into those dreary old dorms."

"How could I leave all this luxury?" Miranda said with a slight, rueful laugh as she looked up at the slightly crooked ceiling and peeling paint in Missy's room.

"I know what you mean," Missy agreed. "It is a great place. It's got real charm. Still, you've got to leave the house sometime. Hard as it might be to walk out beyond the walls of the palace."

Miranda shook her head.

Missy nodded. "Okay, suit yourself. But you've got to stop moping like this. It's not healthy. No guy's worth it. Besides, frowning gives you wrinkles. You don't want to have to Botox before your time."

Miranda sighed. She wanted to explain that it wasn't the guy she was missing, it was the music. She hadn't picked up a pair of sticks since she'd left the shop. She knew she could probably find another teacher, but she'd never find another place to practice. And unless she could play regularly, she'd never get good enough to apply to the school of music. So it was probably better just to move on. Maybe she'd take a few journalism classes. She'd always been a pretty decent writer.

"Oh, my God, I have the best news!" Kathleen shouted, running up the stairs at top speed and into Missy's room. "I am *so* happy!"

"Let me guess—Courtney Love named you her shopping guru!" Missy teased.

Kathleen rolled her eyes. "Oh, please. She's gone so Hollywood. I'd rather dress Mother. No, this is *huge.*"

"They opened a new piercing shop in the neighborhood," Missy tried.

"No. Besides, you know I wouldn't trust my piercings to anyone but Spider."

Miranda made a face. Somehow she wouldn't trust *anything* to a guy named Spider. Especially not holes in her body. "Come on, tell us. What happened?" she asked Kathleen.

"Charlie got mono!" Kathleen was practically squealing with delight, which was completely out of character for her. Punks didn't usually squeal. They kind of grunted.

Miranda and Missy stared at Kathleen. "Some kid is lying in bed, unable to lift his head, and that's *good* news?" Missy asked.

"Uh-huh," Kathleen said. "The *best.* Especially for Miranda."

"Me?" Miranda demanded, shocked. "What did I have to do with it?"

"Yeah, what did she have to do with Charlie getting the kissing disease?" Missy asked, obviously intrigued by the juiciness of the possibilities.

"Hey, don't blame me. I don't even *know* Charlie," Miranda told her.

"Charlie's the drummer in Sin-Phony," Kathleen explained. She smiled even more broadly. "*Now* do you get it?"

The girls stared at her blankly.

"You guys are so dense!" Kathleen exclaimed. "Charlie has to go home for the fall semester. That leaves Sin-Phony without a drummer . . . and Miranda here is a drummer without a band."

"Oh Kathleen, I don't think so," Miranda told her. "I've only been playing for a summer. The guys in Jay's band have been playing for years."

"They're not so great," Kathleen

assured Miranda. "They're just having fun."

"But . . . ," Miranda began.

"But nothing. You're dying to play again."

"I'm *really* not. . . ."

"Then why are your fingers tapping like that?"

Miranda looked down. Sure enough, her fingers were picking up a beat on a notebook that was lying on Missy's bed.

"Okay, so your audition is on Tuesday," Kathleen continued. "Meet me here right after your three o'clock class and we'll head over to the studio where Sin-Phony practices."

"This Tuesday?" Miranda gasped. "That's just three days away."

"Good. Then you won't have time to get nervous." Kathleen answered.

Too late. "I don't even know what kind of music they play," Miranda told her. "I mean, do you have a tape or something?"

Kathleen shook her head.

"Well, can you ask Jay for one so I can at least *hear* them?"

Again, Kathleen shook her head and bit

her upper lip nervously. "You see . . . the thing is . . . well—"

"Well what?" Miranda demanded.

"The guys don't actually know I've set this thing up for you. I figured you and I would just show up at the band meeting and then you could blow them away with your drumming—"

"You want to *ambush* them into letting me audition for the band?"

"'Ambush' is such a strong word," Kathleen said slowly. "I prefer surprise."

"Yeah well, General Custer thought he was surprising folks too. And look what happened to him," Miranda reminded her.

"Miranda's last band," Missy joked.

"You're not helping . . . ," Kathleen hissed at Missy between clenched teeth. She turned to Miranda. "What've you got to lose?"

"My self-esteem, for starters."

"Self-esteem's overrated."

"Good thing you're not a psych major," Miranda replied. "They tend to take the whole self-esteem thing really seriously."

"Come on," Kathleen said. "You can do this. Besides, you'd be doing me a favor.

With you in the band, I know there'll be someone there keeping her eye on Jay when I'm not around. There's always a bunch of strange girls hanging around the band, you know."

"Sin-Phony has groupies?" Missy sounded surprised. "I didn't know they'd actually played any gigs yet."

"Not yet, but they've got things in the works," Kathleen replied. "And you know, where there's a band, there's bound to be groupies. Which is why I need a spy to infiltrate the band and keep watch on things. Oh, and did I mention that two of the guys in the band are totally single, and really hot? The keyboardist, Bobby, is kind of a classic bad boy—real tough, angry young man on the outside, but sweet on the inside. And Adam's the sensitive-artist type. He writes most of the lyrics for the songs and—"

"Not interested," Miranda replied adamantly. "I'm swearing off men for a while."

"All right. But you don't have to swear off drumming, too. So come on, Miranda, what do you say?"

"You'll be there for the audition?" Miranda asked Kathleen, her defenses slowly breaking down.

Kathleen nodded. "Wouldn't miss it." She picked up two pencils and placed one in each of Miranda's hands.

Instantly her long fingers curled around them as though they were drumsticks. Miranda sighed. It did feel good to have her hands wrapped around two sticks again, even if they were just number-two pencils. If nothing else, at least she'd have a chance to be behind a drum set again. "All right, I'll give it a shot," she said finally.

Later that night, Miranda picked up her cell phone and dialed Cally's number. It had been a long time since she'd heard a voice from home, even if that voice was actually hundreds of miles away in California. Two rings went by, and then Miranda could hear Cally's familiar, cheerful voice on the other end.

"Hello?"

"Cal? It's me. Miranda."

"Hey Rand, howya doin?"

"Okay, I guess."

"You guess?"

Miranda sighed. "I'm just a little out of sorts, is all."

"So go find that twenty-five-year-old drummer dude of yours, and have him put everything back in place," Cally teased.

Miranda sighed. As predicted, Cally had definitely been impressed by Paul's age. Too bad he'd acted more like a kid than the man he was. "No can do, Cal," Miranda told her. "He's out of the picture."

"Oh. I'm sorry," Cally said sincerely. "So I guess you're not drumming much anymore."

"I wasn't, for a little while," Miranda admitted. "But I'm going to start up again. I might be trying out for a band."

"A band!" Cally exclaimed. "Whoa. Awesome. What kind of band? Are you going to be a rocker chick, or a country drummer or . . ."

"I don't know," Miranda admitted. "I . . . um . . . I guess I'll find out when I get to the audition." Audition. Just the sound of the word made her kind of shake inside. She needed to change the subject. "So, how's L.A.?"

"Unbelievable," Cally told her. "Gorgeous. Nothing like home. There are palm trees, and beaches, and of course lots and lots of malls!"

"Your kind of town," Miranda said, laughing.

"Yeah. And the people are really wild. Tonight, some of the kids on my dorm floor and I did the coolest thing. We went to hear a channeler."

"A what?"

"A *channeler*," Cally repeated. "He's this really spiritual dude who goes into a big trance, and then channels the spirit of an ancient Chinese mystic. It's the wildest thing, Rand. He's this young guy, probably not more than twenty-three or twenty-four. But when he's in the trance, his voice changes and his body movements become just like an old man's. He went on and on about his philosophy of life, and how it was an ever-evolving cycle—that change is inevitable. I'm telling you, it was the most incredible experience. The best twenty-five dollars I've ever spent."

Miranda didn't know what surprised her the most: the fact that the usually logical, down-to-earth Cally had spent twenty-five bucks to hear an obvious phony pretend to bring back the spirit of a dead guy, or the fact that she'd used the phrase "spiritual dude." Either way, Cally had definitely changed since getting to California just three weeks ago.

Then again, Miranda had done some changing too. Change *was* inevitable. Miranda could see that. And it hadn't even cost her twenty-five dollars to figure it out.

Eight

Without a pad kit to bang on——there was
no way she was asking Paul for that back——
Miranda had to find other ways to practice
for the audition. She created a sort of
makeshift drum set out of different-size
plastic garbage cans and lids. Her roommates were being kind about her practicing, especially considering that the plastic
made more noise than the pad kit ever did.
They knew it was only for a few days. After
that, Miranda would either practice with
the band at their studio, or . . . she didn't
want to even consider the alternative. The
power of positive thinking, that was the
trick.

At least for the time being, she was drumming again. And she found that it was kind of cool playing outside. There was a wild sound that came from the hollow plastic cans, very raw and urban. Although it was a drag when a strong wind came along and blew her bass drum or high hat off the porch in the middle of a good rhythm. And then there was the matter of the lady who lived next door. She kept opening her window and screaming at Miranda with words that would make a sailor blush. Still, so far she hadn't called the noise police or anything, so Miranda just ignored her.

Kathleen had managed to sneak a Sin-Phony demo tape out of Jay's room on Saturday afternoon, while he was busy napping. It turned out that despite Jay's taste in clothing and girlfriends, the band wasn't punk at all. Theirs was a more unique Texas kind of sound, a blend of country and R & B, with just a drop of Tejano influence. It was a sound Miranda could appreciate. She was especially fond of some of the lyrics.

So by the time Tuesday came around,

Miranda was as prepared as she could be. As soon as her class was over, she hurried back to the house and changed into comfortable clothes—a red and white tank top, a plain pair of Levi's, and sneakers. Her Frye boots probably would have looked better, but she was more comfortable drumming in sneakers. It was easier to keep the feel of the bass drum's foot pedal.

"You ready?" Kathleen asked as Miranda came bounding down the stairs, sticks in hand.

"As I'll ever be," Miranda replied, sounding less than sure.

"You're going to be great."

Miranda frowned. "Are you sure they haven't gotten a drummer yet?"

"Positive," Kathleen assured her. "They're meeting today to discuss the whole sitch. So we're getting in there before the rush."

Miranda gulped. She hadn't anticipated there being a rush. She could be up against some really experienced musicians. She probably didn't have a chance.

"Relax," Kathleen told her. "Just go

have fun. Wait'll you see the drum set at the studio. It's awesome."

"Whose drum set is it?"

"It belongs to the studio. It's part of the rental fee for the room."

Miranda nodded. She grew quiet, not saying a word as they took the bus downtown, finally getting off near Congress Avenue. She followed Kathleen down a small side street and into an older building that housed about ten soundproof studios in its three stories. Sin-Phony was practicing on the second floor.

"Hey guys," Kathleen said, stepping into the studio.

"Babe," Jay greeted her. "What're you doing here?"

"Kat, this is a band meeting. No guests. And that includes girlfriends," Bobby, the keyboardist for the band, groaned. He ran his hand through his Mohawk. "We got a real emergency, and we gotta deal with it now. Y'all have to leave."

"That's why I'm here, Bobby," Kathleen replied. "I've got your drummer."

"Really?" Jay jumped up, suddenly

sounding far more glad to see his girl-friend. "Who is he?"

"Not he, *she,*" Kathleen replied. "Here's your new drummer."

All eyes turned toward Miranda.

"*She's* a drummer?" Bobby blurted out.

"A good one," Kathleen assured him.

"Uh, Kat, can I talk to you for a moment?" Jay asked, pulling her aside.

Miranda was becoming more and more uncomfortable with each passing minute. She looked from Jay to Bobby and back again. With their dark punky outfits, matching Mohawks, and similar pissed-off expressions, they could have been mirror images of each other. For a moment, Miranda wondered how Kathleen could ever tell she'd wound up with the right one. They were like the Bobbsey Twins of bar bands—and they both seemed to be staring at Miranda with disdain. She had to fight the urge to turn and run out of the room. If Adam, the bass player—a tall, lanky guy with chin-length, straight dark hair, and soulful brown eyes, who Miranda vaguely remembered talking to at the party they'd had at the house—hadn't given her a gentle smile, she most certainly would have. But that single show of kindness was enough to steel her and keep her in the room.

"She just doesn't seem like the kind of drummer we're looking for," Jay told Kathleen in a voice loud enough for the others to hear. "We need a wild man. An animal."

"You haven't even heard her play," Kathleen told him. "She's plenty wild."

"Come on," Jay replied. "I know Miranda. She's a sweet kid. But she's kinda quiet. I've been at your house a thousand times since she moved in, and I don't think she's said two words to me. And she hasn't exactly been playing a long time."

"No. But she's a natural. You gotta hear her, Jay."

Jay shook his head and walked over to Miranda. "Look kid, I don't want to hurt your feelings or anything, but we're looking to get some gigs. And we need someone who . . . who . . . well, someone who goes crazy behind the skins."

Miranda gulped and blinked her eyes. She wasn't quite sure how to answer that.

Luckily, Adam jumped into the fray for her. "Hey man, give her a chance," he said. "Let her jam with us on a few tunes. What's it gonna hurt?"

"My thoughts exactly," Kathleen agreed.

Bobby and Jay looked at each other. Finally, Bobby stepped behind the keyboard. Jay picked up his Fender and started to tune the strings. Adam grabbed his left-handed bass and plucked out a short, rhythmic combination.

"All right, but just one tune," Jay agreed.

Miranda went and nervously sat behind the drum set in the back of the studio. Her heart was pounding so hard, she wasn't sure she'd be able to follow any other rhythm. She bit her lower lip and tried to remember how to breathe.

Luckily, the studio drum set was a style she was familiar with: a bass drum, rack tom-tom, floor tom-tom, snare drum, ride cymbal, and a crash cymbal. A "Ringo set," was what Paul had called it, referring to the basic, simple setup the Beatles' drummer, Ringo Starr, had used when touring with the band in the 1960s.

"Let's try 'Same Old, Same Old,'" Jay

said. "A-one, two—a-one, two, three . . ."

The band broke into one of the tunes from the contraband tape Kathleen had sneaked to Miranda, so she was familiar with the tune—a mix of hard rock and country. She played with all her heart, her shyness disappearing as the beat took over her very being. It was amazing how at one she was with the drums, her arms and feet moving as though they had minds of their own. By the time the song was over, her heart was pounding, and beads of sweat had formed on her face.

"Not bad," Jay had to admit.

"*Not bad?*" Kathleen demanded. "She was awesome. Wild!"

"I don't know," Bobby said. "She's okay, but a *chick* in our band?"

"Could bring in more fans," Kathleen suggested.

"More fans?" Adam laughed. "How about *any* fans?"

"I'm not sure," Jay said slowly. "She's so new. Kinda raw."

"Raw's a good thing," Kathleen argued. "No one thought the Sex Pistols could play a lick, but—"

"This isn't punk music—," Jay reminded her.

"Well, I vote yes," Adam interrupted. "I'm the other half of the rhythm section, and I think I can work with her."

Miranda looked over at him and smiled gratefully. It was weird having them talk about her as if she weren't in the room, but at least Adam was saying something nice.

"But we haven't even heard anyone else," Bobby reminded him, scratching one of the buzz-cut sides of his head.

"Oh yeah, like people are gonna be banging down the door to audition for a band that hasn't played any gigs yet," Adam replied. "Let's face it, man, we're not looking for a recording contract. All we want to do is play music for a bunch of drunken college kids. If Miranda here is willing to help kick in for the studio time, I say let's go for it. Besides, I hear she's a kick-butt basketball player—with her around, we can get back to playing two on two again after rehearsals." He gave her a quick wink.

Miranda looked up at him, surprised that he'd even remembered the conversation about basketball they'd had at the party.

"Well, it *is* only for a semester, till Charlie gets back," Jay said. He turned to Miranda. "We each kick in ten bucks for each practice session. And we practice four times a week. Can you do that?"

Miranda thought. Forty dollars a week. Five more than her lessons with Paul had been. She'd have to eat generic mac and cheese at least four nights a week and stop calling Cally so often. Long distance sure did add up.

"Maybe you could ask your folks for a few extra bucks a month," Kathleen suggested, noting Miranda's quiet anxiety.

Miranda shook her head. She wasn't about to tell them she was spending her evenings playing rock music with three guys in a small dark studio space. "My parents? No. Things are pretty strapped for them as it is."

"Oh," Jay said. "Well, the thing is, we sort of have to split this four ways, or else it's too much cash for the rest of us."

"No, that's okay. I'll be able to swing it," she said finally.

"Cool," Adam said. "Welcome to Sin-Phony."

"Thanks," she said, giving all three of the guys a big grin.

Adam was the only one who grinned back. Miranda sighed. Well, at least she had *one* ally. Whole wars had been won with less than that.

Nine

Adam was so focused on the notepad in front of him that he didn't even hear Miranda enter the studio. She watched him from the doorway for a moment, his head bent so intently over the paper, his long, straight hair just barely grazing the table as he scribbled words on the page. She waited until he seemed to have written all the words he had in his head, and then entered the room.

"Howdy," she greeted him, walking over to the bench where he was sitting.

"Oh hey, Miranda, how's it goin'?"

"Okay, I guess. I just finished the world's most difficult composition: a compare-and-contrast piece on books by Hemingway and Fitzgerald."

"Wow. That's a tough one. They're both pretty complicated writers. An essay like that probably took a lot of thought."

Miranda sighed. "I used to love writing in high school, but this composition class is taking all the fun out of it. I just sit there in front of my computer and stare at a blank screen for hours." She glanced down at the pad on the table. "You sure don't seem to have any trouble writing."

Adam shrugged. "Depends on the day. Today's a good one. But sometimes I just sit and stare at the paper too."

"So what're you working on?" Miranda asked, trying to take a peek.

"Um, it's not finished yet," Adam replied, hurriedly removing the pad from the table and tucking it into his guitar case. "What are you doing here so early?" he asked, changing the subject.

"I thought I'd work out a few cymbal ideas on that new song, 'Massacre of the Heart,'" she replied. "I'm not totally happy with what I've got going. And it's such a great song. I want to do it justice."

Adam smiled. "It's nice to hear some-one say they want to work on one of my songs. I've got to tell you, you've been jam-ming with us for two weeks, but already you're doing more interesting things with my songs than Charlie ever did."

Miranda blushed. "Thanks," she mur-mured quietly.

After that, they stood there for a moment, just sort of staring into space. Neither one of them was the type of person to just make random conversation, so the room just grew kind of quiet; almost uncomfortable.

"Tell ya what," Adam said, finally breaking the silence. "How about you and I jam on 'Massacre' for a while, together?"

Miranda nodded. "I'd sure appreciate that." She pulled a pair of sticks from the long, thin black case in her backpack and sat down behind the drums.

"No problem. It's always better to fig-ure things out with someone else. Working in a vacuum's no fun at all."

Miranda smiled. She was glad Adam was in Sin-Phony. He was always so kind to her, even protective. Sort of like the big brother she'd never had. It was he who defended her when Jay and Bobby made cracks about girls not being able to cut it on the Austin music scene—throwing out names like Janis Joplin, the sixties blues icon who had made a name for herself in the Texas capital, singing at clubs like Threadgills.

"Okay, let's take it from Jay's chorus," Adam said. He began plucking at the strings of bass, forming a strong, constant rhythm that took over the room. Miranda joined in, following his lead, and then taking over, setting the pace for a while.

"My heart's been crushed, and I don't know if it will rise again," Adam sang out as they played. It was Jay's vocal, but Miranda liked the way Adam sang it better. When Jay did the chorus, it sounded angry and cold—sort of a male version of Alanis Morissette. But Adam sang it more mournfully, as though the pain were real.

Just then, Bobby and Jay came racing excitedly into the studio. Instantly the vibe in the room switched. "Y'all are never gonna believe this!" Bobby shouted. "It's totally *un*believeable."

"You're not kidding, bro," Jay agreed.

"What?" Adam asked.

"You won't be able to guess," Bobby continued.

"So tell me."

"Come on, don't you want to guess?" Bobby asked Adam. He sounded disappointed.

"We got a gig?" Miranda suggested.

Bobby's face resembled a deflated balloon. "How'd you guess?" he demanded.

Miranda looked away, sorry for stealing his thunder. "I . . . uh . . . I was just being hopeful."

"Well, you're right," Jay told her. "We got a gig at Sally's Pub."

"No way!" Adam exclaimed. "Sally's? How'd we get that?"

"We bugged the manager till she said yes," Bobby replied.

"Actually, I had to promise her that Bobby would quit asking her out if she let us play," Jay joked. "He's been a real pain to her."

Miranda nodded. Jay's tone may have been teasing, but knowing Bobby, there was probably more than a grain of truth to the story.

"Wow, Sally's," Adam mused. "That's pretty cool." He looked over at Miranda, realizing that she'd only been in town a few months and wasn't as familiar with the scene as they were. "It's a little club on Red River Street," he told her, "but it's always packed with kids from the colleges. Mostly because the beer's cheap."

"Yeah well, they might come for cheap beer, but once they hear us jammin', they'll stay for the music," Bobby boasted.

Jay laughed. "Let's hope."

"Wait a minute," Miranda interrupted. "I can't play at Sally's."

"Excuse me?" Jay said.

"I told you, you can't trust chicks," Bobby butted in.

"It's not my fault," Miranda insisted. "It's just that I don't actually own a drum set. I'm using the studio's kit, remember?"

"Oh, that's no big deal," Jay assured her. "Sally's has a house kit. It's too big a pain to drag drums all over Austin. All the drummers use the house kit. You're cool."

"Oh, good," Miranda replied, relieved.

"So when's the gig?" Adam asked.

"Next Wednesday night," Jay told him.

"So we've got to get practicing. We really want to be smokin' for our big debut." He sighed. "Too bad Charlie's missing this."

Miranda bit her lip and slumped down a bit. She felt as though she'd stolen something from the other drummer. But Adam was willing to give credit where it was due. "I think Miranda's our lucky charm," he told the other guys.

"How do you figure?" Bobby asked.

"We didn't get any gigs before she showed up on the scene. Now, Sally just picked us up. And it was the *new* tape she heard—the one with Miranda on it—wasn't it?"

Jay nodded.

"Yeah well, whatever," Bobby interjected, unwilling to accept that Miranda—or any girl—might have anything to do with this. "She can have all the guys at Sally's. But the women are for us. Oh, this is gonna be awesome. You know how girls love musicians." He raised his hand to his head. "I've got to get a new buzz on the sides. I want to look good for the gals."

Jay laughed. "Like that's gonna help. Forget it, man. Women love lead singers.

All eyes are gonna be on me. And I'm gonna give those girls one hell of a show." He swiveled his hips slightly, like a bad Elvis imitator.

Miranda frowned, and for a moment, she thought about bringing up Kathleen's name, just to remind Jay that he already had a girlfriend. But she changed her mind. She was already pretty much an unwelcome intruder in the band. No point making things worse.

"How much are we making?" Adam asked.

"Well . . . that's the thing," Bobby began.

"Actually, we're not getting paid any-thing—*this time*," Jay explained. "It's sort of a trial outing. But if they like us, then next time we'll get a piece of the door."

"And we get all the beer and groupies we can handle," Bobby added. "Once the girls hear us, that'll all fall into place."

"Yeah well, there's gonna be no one there to listen to us if we stink up the place," Adam reminded them. "Which we'll do if we don't get some practicing in. Miranda and I were just working on

'Massacre of the Heart.' Why don't we start with that?"

"Cool," Jay replied, taking his ax from the case and strapping it over his shoulder.

As Bobby began the keyboard intro to the song, Miranda looked up gratefully at Adam. She was glad he'd gotten them back to the music.

"You need a lift home?" Adam asked Miranda as they walked out of the studio after the rehearsal.

"Oh, that would be awesome," Miranda thanked him. "The buses take so long at night." She looked around. "Where's your car?"

"Who said anything about a car?" Adam asked her. He walked over to the big red and black motorcycle that was parked in front of the studio entrance.

"You mean on a motorcycle?" Miranda asked nervously. That explained why he'd given Bobby his bass to take back to the apartment they shared. He couldn't have carried it home on this thing. "I didn't know you had a bike."

Adam grinned. "There's a lot of things

you don't know about me, Miranda."

"Oh, well . . . I . . . um . . ." She didn't know what to say. She'd never been on a motorcycle before. It seemed so huge and forbidding. What if it turned over or something?

"A first timer?" Adam asked, smiling.

Miranda wrinkled her nose. "It shows, huh?"

"Oh yeah," Adam teased. "But don't sweat it. There's a first time for everything." He threw her a black helmet. "Here, put this on. Safety first."

She sighed nervously, fingering the leather strap at the base of the helmet. "Don't worry," Adam assured her. "I'm a good driver. I'll take care of you. I don't want anything to happen to the other half of our rhythm section." He leaped onto the bike. "Just get on behind me and put your arms around my waist." She did as she was told. "That's it," Adam continued. "Now, hold on tight. Move your body in the same direction I do."

And with that, he turned the key in the ignition. Miranda could feel the bike vibrating beneath her, and then, with a loud revving of the engine, they took off down the road. At first, Miranda's body was stiff and unsure, and she could feel her heart pounding wildly. But as Adam continued to drive smoothly down the empty side streets, she felt herself relax. It was hard not to, what with the wind blowing on her face and the streetlights just sort of zooming by before her eyes. There was an excitement about being on the back of a motorcyle—sort of like cantering on a horse through the woods, but much smoother and a whole hell of a lot faster. The ride was just dangerous enough to give her whole body a thrill. In fact, she was totally bummed when Adam pulled up in front of her house.

"Okay, we're here," he told her, leaping off the bike and helping her down.

"That was fun," Miranda told him.

"I told you you'd love it," Adam reminded her. "Wait, you'll see. Before long, you'll want a bike of your own."

"Oh I'm not so sure about that," Miranda disagreed. "But I liked being on the back of yours. You're a good driver."

"Tell my mom that," Adam joked. "She

worries all the time about my being on this thing."

Miranda didn't doubt it. Mothers were like that. "Well, I'll be glad to vouch for you."

"Thanks," Adam said, flashing her a sparkling grin as he hopped back on the bike. "I think you and I are gonna get along just fine. See ya at rehearsal."

Miranda waved as he drove off. It was nice to know she had a friend in the band.

"Whoa, Sally's Pub, huh?" Kathleen exclaimed. "That's pretty good. The guys must be so psyched."

Miranda, Kat, and Missy were gathered in the living room later that evening. They were celebrating over a huge container of Cherry Garcia ice cream.

"Oh, it's going to be so amazing," Miranda agreed, folding her legs under her and digging her spoon into the carton.

"I'll bet Bobby and Adam are already considering the groupie effect this gig'll have," Kathleen said, laughing. "You know how single guys can be."

Miranda took a deep breath. She was

tempted to tell Kathleen that it was Bobby and *Jay,* not Adam, who seemed consumed with the idea of female fans. But she thought better of it. Despite the fact that Kathleen had wanted her in the band to keep an eye on Jay, Miranda didn't really want to get in the middle. "Bobby's a piece of work," she murmured, filling her mouth with ice cream so she couldn't say anything else.

A moment later, her cell phone began to jingle its strange mechanical tune. *Saved by the bell,* she thought as she pulled the phone from her pocket and headed into the next room for privacy. "Howdy," she said, swallowing a piece of frozen cherry.

"Hey sugar, how're ya doin?" her mom's cheery voice rang out at the other end. "Daddy and I just got back from the Cougars' game. Made me think of my little girl. Daddy used to be able to drag you to those games. Now that you're in Austin, I'm his victim."

Miranda laughed. The Cougars were Barton High's football team. Her dad never missed one of their games. He'd played football for the Cougars when he was a teen, and his loyalty had never waivered. His favorite thing to do in high school was show Denny and the other guys in their crowd his bum knee and brag about how little cartilage was left in it. If they were lucky, he'd pop the knee for them.

"So how'd the Cougars do?" Miranda asked her mom.

"Don't ask," her mother said, sighing. "It was pitiful. That's why I called you. For some good news."

Well, there was the gig at Sally's. But Miranda wasn't ready to spring the whole band thing on her mom just yet. "Well, let's see. I'm not going to ask you for any money," she teased instead.

Her mom laughed. "That is good news. How about your classes?"

"College is tougher than high school," Miranda admitted. "But I'm not doing too badly. I got a B plus on my sociology critique, and my English Comp prof seems to like my writing."

"Great!" her mom sounded genuinely pleased. "And how about calculus?"

"Well, that one's a struggle. But I'll be able to pull through it with a B."

"I have no doubt," her mother said. "You can do anything you put your mind to. Always could. You know, Dad and I were talking the other night about your choosing a major. Now I know you don't have to do that until next year. . . ."

Miranda gulped. This was just the kind of conversation she'd been trying to avoid.

"But we were thinking maybe you'd like to take a few advertising classes," her mom continued. "You're such a good writer, and we could sure use your help with that in the landscaping business. It's getting pretty competitive. Wouldn't hurt to have a daughter who could step in and put our name out there."

Miranda sighed. Advertising? Landscaping? Moving back to Barton? That wasn't in her plans at all. Still, her parents were sacrificing plenty to keep her in school. Didn't she owe them something for that? On the other hand, she owed herself a chance at happiness too.

Miranda definitely had a lot of big decisions to make. But it was too much for tonight. She decided to let it pass. "That's a good idea, Mom," she said. "I'll look into it." There. That was good. She hadn't lied. She *would* look into it. That didn't mean she'd take the class.

But as she hung up the phone a few minutes later, she felt sort of guilty. What a night. An evening of lies by omission. First to Kathleen, and then to her mom. Lying wasn't something that came naturally to Miranda. It always tore her up inside.

It was all for the music, she told herself. But somehow, that didn't make her feel any better.

Ten

Rehearsal on Monday night did not go well. Bobby and Jay kept trying to grab the spotlight, each adding so much new flair to their performances that they threw the whole feeling of the band off. Even Adam, to a lesser extent, seemed keen on making the bass the centerpiece of the group. It was what Miranda's dad would call a pissing match—and it was ruining the sound the group had put together.

When rehearsal ended, Bobby and Jay were eager to get out of the studio. "I need a brew," Bobby announced. "When I sound that great, I need to celebrate."

"Me too," Jay agreed. "My voice was so

on. I couldn't believe I finally hit that high note in 'Same Old, Same Old.' I never reach that thing."

"Yeah, but you were off a beat in 'Coldhearted Queen,'" Bobby reminded him.

"Like you didn't miss the first three notes of 'Texas Trilogy,'" Jay countered.

Miranda frowned as they left the room. The guys were so busy bouncing the testosterone around, they hadn't even noticed how badly the band had sounded.

"Nervous?" Adam asked as he placed his bass gently in its case.

Miranda turned around. "Does it show?"

"Mmm. You're more quiet than usual, that's all," Adam told her.

"Yeah, that's how I get when I'm nervous," Miranda admitted. "It's just that I haven't performed anywhere before."

"Not even in those little ballet recitals girls have when they're kids?" Adam asked her.

Miranda shook her head. "I played soccer."

"High school musical?"

"Nope. I was stage crew. Always behind the scenes."

Adam grinned. "Then it's time you got in the spotlight. You've got nothing to worry about, Miranda. You sounded great tonight. Better than the three of us, that's for sure."

So he had noticed. "We just have to work together as a team," Miranda said.

"And there's no 'I' in team, right?" Adam asked.

Miranda laughed. "My dad always says that."

"Mine too. He played basketball in high school."

"Mine played football."

"Hometown heroes," Adam laughed. "They're all alike."

Miranda wanted to ask him more about his hometown, suddenly realizing she knew almost nothing about him. She and the guys in the band never talked about anything other than their music. For the first time, she was actually curious about one of her bandmates. She just didn't know what kind of questions it would be okay to ask him. *Band protocol, and all that.*

Adam grew quiet for a minute, thinking. "You know what'll get rid of that stage fright?"

"What?"

"Eliminating the unknown. What you're imagining is always worse than the real thing. Let's go over to Sally's Pub. Once you see what a little joint it is, I think you'll be a lot less stressed. Come on. My bike's parked right outside."

His plan sounded pretty logical. Besides, she was itching for another ride on his motorcycle. "Okay. But just for a little while. I have three sociology chapters to read before Wednesday."

"A little while is all it'll take," Adam assured her.

Adam was right: Sally's Pub was nothing like what Miranda had imagined. It was really small and dingy. More like a neighborhood bar than a club. There were about twenty tables set up in the big, dark open space. One whole wall was set aside for the bar. Three bartenders stood behind, setting customers up with drinks—mostly draft beers. The stage, which was really nothing more than a rickety wooden platform, was about half the size of the bar. There was a small wooden dance floor right in front of it.

Miranda glanced at the drums that were set up onstage. Sally's Pub's house drum set wasn't anything great. Just a small kit with heavily beaten heads and some old cymbals. She'd be glad to hear it played, though, to see how the thing sounded. "When does the band go on?" she asked Adam.

"I don't know. Soon, I guess. It's almost nine o'clock. Let's get a table in the back. It can get pretty loud if you sit up front."

Miranda nodded and followed him toward the back of the pub. She looked over at the sign over the door: PLEASE LEAVE YOUR FIREARMS OUTSIDE. Miranda gulped slightly. That didn't sound too great. What kind of crowd was hanging out at this place, anyway?

As she took a closer look, Miranda felt strangely overdressed—which was saying a lot, considering she was wearing an old gray T-shirt and a pair of jeans. But the fact that she was actually wearing a shirt that covered her belly button and jeans that didn't slide below the top of her butt made her stand out in this place. It was amazing to her just how little some of the girls were wearing. And, to be perfectly frank, it wasn't like the Britney Spears wannabees actually looked good in their outfits. Most of them just couldn't pull it off—particularly the girl who was currently bending over to tie her shoe. Her rather large derriere was literally hanging out over the top of her low-slung, plus-size jeans. *Further proof some people didn't have full-length mirrors.*

Bang!

Suddenly, a gunshot went off. Miranda leaped up and grabbed Adam. "Oh, my God!" she shouted. "Let's get out of here!"

Adam wrapped a long, protective arm around her and began to laugh. "Easy, girl. It's just a cap gun. Someone's havin' a shooter." He turned her around so she could get a good look at the waitress at a table across the way. She was putting the cap gun back in her holster, and getting ready to pour shots for the guys at the table. "It's just a gimmick to get people to buy overpriced shots," Adam explained.

"It's sure working at that table. Those guys are loaded."

Miranda stared at them. They did seem drunk, especially the guy wearing a weird, hard-plastic helmet equipped with two beer can holders. The holders had straws connected to them that went right toward his mouth. That way, the guy could drink two beers at one time without using his hands—which left him free to pick up the shot glass.

Adam noticed her staring. "Real classy, huh?" he joked. "Not something you'd see in *Vogue*."

"It's a look," Miranda agreed.

"He pulls it off well, don't you think?" Adam walked over to an empty table and pulled a chair out for her.

She looked at him, surprised. No one had ever done that for her before. "Thanks," she murmured.

"You want a beer?"

Miranda shook her head. "Underage," she reminded him. The last thing she needed was to get thrown out of the same bar where she was supposed to play a gig. "I'll just have a club soda."

Their drinks came rather quickly, and Miranda downed hers. She hadn't realized quite how thirsty she was. But Adam sipped his beer slowly, not like Jay and Bobby, who always seemed to drink theirs in rapid time. He was like that in a lot of ways—more cautious and relaxed than the other two. She couldn't for the life of her figure out how he had wound up in the same band with them.

Then again, a few months ago, Miranda wouldn't have pictured herself in a band *at all*! And she probably wouldn't have had friends like Kathleen or Missy.

"Howdy gang! We're Assault and Battery!" the lead singer—a fat, sweaty guy in brown cords, a ripped Willie Nelson T-shirt, and long, unshaped hair—leaped onto the stage and shouted wildly into the mike. "Get ready for the attack!"

Miranda frowned as the music—*if you could call it that*—started. It was hard to make a whole lot of sense of the cacophony that was going on on the stage. The timing was all off. The bass player and the drummer seemed to be playing different songs, while the lead guitarist—a tall, lanky dude

146

in black leather pants and nothing else—seemed to be spending more time thrusting his crotch in the direction of a table of girls than focusing on the chords.

And the lead singer! Well, there wasn't a whole lot to be said about him except he seemed to mistake screaming for singing. And everytime he shook his head, beads of sweat flew off into the audience, showering the people standing directly in front of the stage. Miranda winced as his voice hit a particularly painful note at the exact same time that a fresh wave of feedback burst out of the guitarist's amp.

"Well, all right!" the lead singer shouted as he dove from the stage into the small, drunken crowd before him. But instead of catching him, the group of onlookers parted, leaving the singer a clear path to the hard wooden floor below. He landed with a crash and lay there, completely still. He was knocked out, cold, but his band didn't seem to notice. They just kept on playing whatever it was they were trying to play.

"Seen enough?" Adam asked Miranda.

She nodded.

"Cool. Whaddaya say we go shoot a few hoops, then?"

"Sounds good to me. Anything to get away from this noise."

Adam grinned. "See, I told ya you'd feel better after seeing the place—and hearing one of the regular bands."

"You're not kidding," Miranda replied. "Even at our worst, Sin-Phony sounds better than this."

Adam laughed. "Yeah. Only we're not gonna be at our worst. We're gonna kick ass on Wednesday night."

Miranda smiled confidently. Something in the way Adam said that made her truly believe it.

Unfortunately, that sense of calm didn't last. By Wednesday evening, Miranda was a bundle of nerves again. "I can't do this," she whispered to Kathleen, not two minutes before the band was ready to go on. "I'm heading home. Tell the guys I'm sorry." She wasn't kidding.

"Oh no, you don't," Kathleen said, wrapping a protective arm around Miranda and steering her toward the stage. "You've worked too hard."

"But there are a lot of people here."

"That's a *good* thing, Rand." She reached up and adjusted Miranda's Stetson slightly so the brim leaned back a bit, showing her face.

"No, it's not a good thing at all. I don't want them all to be witnesses."

"To what?"

"To my destruction of this band. I think my hands are numb. I can't play. I don't even remember *how* to play."

"Come on, Miranda," Jay called from beside the stage. "Move it. We're on."

There was no backing out now. Miranda moved toward the stage as though in a trance. She knew there were people around her, but they all seemed fuzzy—like the background actors in a movie. She could see them, sort of hear the murmur of them talking, but she wasn't able to really make out who they were.

She sat down behind the drums and stared out into the audience, trying to imagine everyone in their underwear—like on that old episode of *The Brady Bunch*. But it didn't work. This was no sitcom. This was real life, and everything wasn't going to turn out okay in just thirty minutes, minus time for commercials. She was going to screw this up, in front of all these people. The guys were going to hate her forever, Bobby was going to be proven right about chick drummers, and she'd have to move home to Barton in shame. . . .

. "All right! Let's make some noise!" Jay shouted wildly into the microphone as he struck the first chord of "Same Old, Same Old."

Miranda would never be able to explain what had happened, but somehow, she was able to play. At first, it was as though her arms and legs were on autopilot, able to do what they had been trained for without any assistance from her. But then she felt herself beginning to relax. She wasn't afraid of the crowd anymore. The drums were her armor. Nothing could hurt her as long as she was behind them.

By the time the band broke into its next number, "Texas Trilogy," Miranda was on fire, playing with such passion that not even Bobby could find fault with her. In fact, it was Bobby himself who suddenly shouted "Drum solo!" into his mike.

Without missing a beat, Miranda went wild, playing a kick-ass solo that had the crowd on its feet, cheering and clapping along. Miranda had no idea how long she was playing with the spotlight firmly focused on her. She was unaware of anything besides the beat of her drum. It was rough, organic, and passionate, a feeling of power and excitement that she would never be able to describe accurately to anyone. And she knew for sure now that there was nothing else she would ever want to do.

The audience didn't want to let them off the stage after their final song. There were cheers, calls for encores, and even a few lighters that lit up around the pub. Finally, it was Sally herself who had to come to the stage and tell the audience that it was time for Sin-Phony to go.

"But don't worry, y'all," the middle-aged bar owner assured the crowd. "We're gonna have these folks back again real soon. I think you'll be seein' lots of Sin-Phony round here!"

The crowd roared again. Miranda and the boys stared at one another. Sally had just promised them a gig—no, *lots* of gigs—in front of all of these people. They were on their way.

"Damn, we were smokin'," Bobby boasted as he packed up his keyboard.

"I don't think we've ever sounded like that," Jay agreed.

Adam turned to Miranda. "Where'd you come up with that solo?"

Miranda shrugged. "I have no idea. It just sort of happened. I heard Bobby tell me to play, and I just did."

"Well, you rocked the place. Did you see the way people were cheering for you?"

"They were cheering for all of us. It was amazing. I can't wait to play again," Miranda replied.

"We should get some new material together," Jay suggested as he fastened the sides of his guitar case. "Write some new tunes."

"Not tonight, you're not," Kathleen said, sidling up beside him and playfully biting the piercings on his earlobe. "Tonight we're gonna celebrate."

"Mmm . . . ," Jay moaned suggestively. "What'd you have in mind?"

"Won't you be surprised," Kathleen told him as she picked up the guitar case and pulled him toward the door. "All I can tell you is, it's gonna be real private."

Miranda smiled to herself. Kathleen was smart to get Jay out of the club as quickly as possible. She obviously knew all about girls and musicians. Probably because that was what had attracted her to Jay in the first place.

Jay didn't seem to have any complaints, though. "See you guys later," he called as he followed her away. "Don't call too early, okay?"

"Cool." Bobby quickly turned his attention from Jay and Kathleen and looked out over the crowd. "There she is," he announced, pointing to a tall, leggy brunette dressed in a denim miniskirt and silver halter.

"There *who* is?" Adam asked.

"Tonight's lucky winner of an evening with a rock star," he said. "That chick's been giving me the eye all night long. Now I'm gonna reward the effort." He turned to Adam. "Looks like she's got some hot friends. Come on, dude. We've got the power. Let's use it."

Adam glanced in Miranda's direction for just a second. "You got a way to get home?" he asked her.

Miranda nodded. "Sure. No sweat. Go have fun."

"Because I can take you back to your house if . . ."

"Don't be silly. You heard Bobby. Use your power."

Adam frowned slightly. "It's pretty late, Rand. Maybe I should drive you back."

"Oh, man," Bobby groaned. "I thought we were gonna party. I knew it would be a downer to have a chick in the band." He didn't seem the least bit concerned that what he was saying might hurt Miranda's feelings.

But it did hurt. A lot. Not that she would let him know that. Guys like Bobby didn't deserve that much satisfaction. "No, it's cool—honest," she assured Adam. "I can take care of myself. Besides, I have . . . plans."

Adam studied her face. "What kind of plans?" he asked her.

"Hey, you're not the only one who can party," Miranda answered, although it was completely untrue. She had no real plans. She just didn't want to be a drag or anything. After all, Adam wasn't *really* her big brother. It wasn't his job to take care of her.

Adam lowered his head and nodded slowly. "No. Of course not," he answered quietly. Then he turned toward Bobby. "Lead the way."

Miranda sat there on the stage for a minute, alone. She looked out over the crowd. She spotted Missy at a back table, making out with a bald-headed guy. Not Roger, though. Miranda could tell, because Roger had a red birthmark on the back of his shaved head and this guy's chrome dome was clear of any markings. Roger must've gotten the old heave-ho. Missy was on to the next guy in the swim team relay.

Bobby and Adam were certainly having a good time. The guys were literally surrounded by women from the bar. Bobby had been right: Chicks sure did love musicians—at least *male* musicians. It didn't seem as though any of the guys in the club were paying her much mind. Not that she'd want them to. These fellas weren't her type. Besides, she'd sworn off men.

Miranda picked up her sticks and headed for the door. She'd take the bus home tonight. Maybe try to call Cally. It was still pretty early in L.A. Then she'd kick back and have her own quiet little celebration. Just her and Mother.

Eleven

"Wow! Look at this place!" Miranda exclaimed as she, Kathleen, Jay, Bobby, and Adam took their seats at the Backyard. She'd never seen anything like the outside amphitheater before. "There must be a million seats here!"

"Only about five thousand," Kathleen said, and laughed. "Math really isn't your best subject, is it?"

"Whatever. It's huge," Miranda countered, scowling slightly at Kathleen's joke. "Besides, I'm getting a B in calc."

"Woohoo, I think we're in the midst of a scholar," Jay teased, yanking gently on Miranda's long blond ponytail.

"Okay, these are our seats," Bobby interrupted, pointing to a row about midway toward the stage. "I can't wait for the show to start."

"Me either. I've only seen one or two of these bands before," Jay noted. "I can't wait to hear the rest of 'em."

"It's all bands that made it big after starting in Austin," Adam explained to Miranda.

"Yeah, and next year, *we'll* be here," Bobby boasted. "Maybe even the opening act."

Miranda smiled. Bobby definitely had big dreams. It was an awfully big jump, going from the opening act at Sally's Pub on Wednesday night to playing at a huge amphitheater like the Backyard. She pulled her jean jacket tightly around her as they walked up the seemingly endless stairs to their seats. Even in Austin, the November wind could bring a bit of a chill to the air.

"I wonder how you get on the bill for something like this," Jay asked.

"You probably need a good agent," Kathleen suggested. "Someone who's really connected. And people have to know who you are." She reached into her backpack and pulled out a wad of colorful papers. "Which is why I plan to leave these on a few seats, in the ladies' room, and maybe on a few windshields after we leave."

Miranda looked over Kathleen's shoulder to see what was on the papers. "Wow!" she exclaimed. "It's us."

"Sure is," Kathleen agreed, handing each of the band members a copy of the flyers she'd printed up. There was a huge picture of the band in the middle of the sheet. Just above the photo she'd typed:

Sin-Phony
Appearing every Wednesday
at Sally's Pub

Below the photo she'd typed up some reviews of the band's performances:

"One hot show!"
"They rock the place!"
"Never heard anything like them!"

"Hey, where'd you get those reviews?" Miranda asked her. "I didn't know any critics had come to hear us. "

"They haven't," Kathleen admitted. "I didn't say the reviews were from *critics*. I just typed up things I heard people say."

"What people?" Bobby asked. "Sounds like we've got some dedicated fans."

"Sure, you do," Kathleen assured him. "Missy said the first one, and that third one's from me. But the *second* one's really from someone who doesn't even know you guys!"

"Truth in advertising. Is that what they're teachin' you at school?" Jay chuckled.

"I'll show you what they're teaching me," she replied as she leaned over and stuck her tongue in his ear.

"Get a room, you guys," Bobby groaned.

Adam turned his attention toward Miranda, who was sitting between him and Kathleen. He smiled at the look of excitement on her face. "I guess they don't have places like this in your hometown either?" he asked.

Miranda shook her head. "We have a lot of little local places, but nothing this big. We're not near any cities, so it's kind of tough to get to the big shows. We used to talk about taking road trips to see some of the bigger bands, but we never got around to it. There was always a football game at school to go to, or our parents nixed it or something."

"Same here. But that was okay, you know. It was worth it. It's kind of great growing up in a small town, huh?"

Miranda nodded. "It was fun. You always feel safe. Everyone knows you. On the other hand, everyone knows your business, too."

Adam laughed. "Oh, yeah," he agreed. He paused for a minute, studying her face with his big brown eyes. "Are you bummed about not going back there for Thanksgiving?"

Miranda frowned. She'd been trying not to think about that. Her parents had been very understanding when she'd told them that since the vacation was just four days, and the bus ride was so long, she'd probably stay in Austin for Thanksgiving. After all, Christmas break came just a few weeks after, and then she'd be home for four whole weeks. It was hard for them to argue with that type of logic.

Of course, Miranda hadn't mentioned the *real* reason she wanted to stay in Austin: The group had a gig at Sally's Pub on Wednesday night. And since all the better-known bands had other plans for Thanksgiving eve, Sin-Phony was headlining! There was no way she was missing that.

"Thanksgiving at home *is* nice," Miranda admitted. "My mom makes a huge turkey, stuffing, cranberries, the whole bit. And all my cousins come from miles around. We shoot hoops in my driveway and . . ."

Adam wrapped a comforting arm around her. "Hey, we're gonna have a great time Wednesday night. Sally's isn't going to know what hit it. Then, on Thursday we can all go for a Thanksgiving dinner. And if you want, we can even shoot a few hoops at the gym to work it off."

Miranda looked at him, surprised. "You're going to be here on Thanksgiving day?"

Adam nodded. "Sure. I never go home on Thanksgiving. Neither does Bobby. Last year, Jay went to Kathleen's folks, but I think this time they're hanging in Austin. So we were planning a band Thanksgiving somewhere really funky this year."

"I can come too?" Miranda asked him.

"You're part of the band, aren't you?"

Miranda smiled. It *was* really starting to feel that way.

Later that evening, Miranda sat in front of her laptop, working on a sociology term paper. It was hard to concentrate. She kept replaying the concert in her mind. There were so many great bands, all styles of music, from rockabilly to salsa to reggae. And the crowd was accepting of all of it. Austin really was the music capital of the world—or at least of Texas, anyway. It made Miranda proud to be a part of it all.

Suddenly her cell began to ring. She picked it up, glancing at the small screen on the top of the phone. The area code was from her hometown, but she didn't recognize the number. "Hello?" she answered curiously.

"Hey, Rand."

She gasped for a moment, recognizing the voice immediately. "Denny?"

"Yeah." He coughed nervously. "How ya doin'?"

"I'm fine," she replied, her voice as nervous as his. "You?"

"Oh, I'm okay. Been busy. I've got school, and of course I'm working at the company. I'm in the dispatch department now, but after Christmas break, Dad's moving me over to sales. I've been working real hard. I'm actually calling from the plant right now."

"Oh," Miranda said, glancing at her watch. It was nearly nine. He was working late. Her mind was racing. Why was Denny calling now, after all these months? Surely he hadn't called to make small talk.

"So how's the weather up there?" he continued. "It was a little chilly today. I had to wear that awful sweater my aunt Janine made for me."

"It's chilly here too," Miranda answered. "I was out all day, though, at one of those outdoor concerts."

"A concert, huh? What kind?"

Oops. Maybe she shouldn't have mentioned the music. She didn't want to let on too much about her life in Austin.

Somehow that didn't seem to be Denny's business. Miranda wanted to keep her two lives separate. Then and now. "Just some local bands. Nothing special." *But it had been special. Incredibly special.*

"Anyhow, the reason I'm calling is your dad told me you weren't comin' home for Thanksgiving," Denny said, changing the subject.

"No. I can't really swing it. I've got lots of work, and classes on Wednesday, so . . ."

"Well, my family's not going to be around either," Denny continued. "They're taking a cruise to Mexico. I didn't want to go, so . . . well . . . I was thinkin' you and I could maybe spend Thanksgiving together in Austin."

The words hit her like a ton of bricks. *Worlds colliding.* "I don't know, Den. I'm really busy. I . . ." She stopped for a minute. This was ridiculous. She hadn't heard from him in five months and now he suddenly invites himself into her home . . . into her life? "What's this all about, Denny?" she demanded.

"I miss you, Rand. Nothing's right without you." The words poured out of his mouth. "And I know you miss me, too."

"Sometimes," she said weakly. It was the truth. Although she'd been thinking about him less and less lately, he did pop into her brain now and again.

"You know, we never really talked after . . . after . . . well, you know, after Cally's party."

"Whose fault was that?"

"Mine, Miranda," he told her, sounding very small and far away. "I know that now. That's why I'm coming to visit. I need to explain."

"There's nothing to explain," Miranda answered flatly. "I understood completely."

"No, you didn't. You couldn't have. Because I didn't understand it. Not till now. That's why I'm coming up. You see, I figured out that you and I have to be together. It's destiny. We're star-crossed lovers."

Miranda sighed. He must have been reading *Romeo and Juliet* in Lit class.

"I've got a class on Wednesday morning, but I'll hop in the car and leave right from school. I can be at your place by three o'clock at the latest."

Wednesday. He couldn't be there Wednesday. That was the night Sin-Phony was headlining at Sally's Pub. The last thing she wanted was for Denny to know she was drumming. He was pretty conservative. It was bad enough she was living in a house with a punk rocker, a sports groupie, and a mannequin. If he knew about her drumming, he'd . . . he'd . . . well, she didn't know what he'd do!

"I can't on Wednesday, Den. I have a . . . um . . . a night class. I won't be back till late."

"A class on the Wednesday night before Thanksgiving? That's cruel."

"You know how professors can be."

"I sure do. I have a few of my own, you know. Anyhow, that's okay, I'll just hang out till you get back from class. "

"But, Denny—"

"No 'buts,' Rand. I'm not takin' no for an answer."

Miranda sighed. When Denny got something stuck in his head, there was no stopping him. So, reluctantly, she gave him the address.

"Got it," he said. "I'll see you in three days, Rand."

"Yeah. See ya," Miranda replied, hanging up the phone. Then she raced toward the stairs. "HELP!" she shouted to her roommates. "HELP!"

Twelve

Tuesday afternoon's rehearsal was a disaster. Miranda's focus wasn't on the music, and everybody knew it. She lost the beat a few times, and had difficulty staying in time with Adam's bass.

"Come on, Miranda, what's up?" Bobby asked, after stopping for the third time in the middle of "Southern Funk," their new song. "You gotta keep your mind on the music."

How could she keep her mind on her music when Denny, the messenger of impending disaster, would be on his way in a few hours? Miranda sighed. Denny wasn't even here yet and already he was causing trouble.

"Well, our rehearsal time's almost up, anyhow," Adam said, once again coming to Miranda's rescue. "And we always sound awful just before a big show. Remember the week before our first gig? Miranda was the only one who sounded good."

She smiled at him gratefully.

"I know what's buggin' her. It's man trouble," Jay teased. "Kathleen told me all about Donny."

"Denny," Miranda corrected him.

"Whatever."

"Who's Donny?" Adam asked. He looked at her strangely. "I didn't know you were seeing anyone, Miranda."

"Denny," Miranda repeated. "And I'm not seeing anyone. Denny's my ex-boyfriend."

"And he's coming to town trying to 'x' the 'ex' out of that title," Jay announced. He was obviously pleased that he knew something Bobby and Adam didn't. *Guys could be the biggest gossips sometimes.*

"Well, it isn't going to work," Miranda assured Jay. "Denny is my past."

"Then let's talk about the future," Adam interrupted. "Say Thursday. What time do y'all want to meet up at Rikyu?"

"Mmm . . ." Bobby laughed. "Sushi for Thanksgiving. Wonder what the Pilgrims would have though about that."

"How about three? I'm planning on sleeping in," Jay said.

"Not with Kathleen around, you're not," Bobby teased.

"Well, we're planning on staying in bed, anyhow," Jay agreed.

"Me too," Bobby said. "I just haven't decided who's gonna be there with me."

"Three sounds good to me," Adam agreed. "Does three o'clock work for you, Miranda?"

She really would have liked to have Thanksgiving dinner with the band. But, now . . . "I'm not going to be able to make it," she told Adam. "Denny's going to be here, and . . ."

"Oh," Adam said, shifting his weight slightly from side to side. "Okay."

"I mean, I would have wanted to come. I was planning on it, and then—"

"Hey, it's cool," Adam told her. "Wednesday night's what's really important, anyway."

"We just have some unfinished business," Miranda continued. "And I want to set him straight on a few things."

"So why not bring him? We'll set him straight for ya," Bobby told her.

"I think that's what she's afraid of. Kathleen says Denny wouldn't be too fond of Miranda making music with three great-looking guys like us," Jay told the others, running his hands through his jet-black Mohawk. "So she's keeping us hidden."

"It's not that," Miranda said feebly. "It's just that Denny's sort of, well, he just wouldn't fit in. That's all." She looked up at Adam. Usually, he was the one who backed her up and gave her support. But this time he was barely looking at her.

"Don't worry about it," Adam said as he hoisted his bass case over his shoulder and headed for the door. "No big deal."

"Oh God, Denny's going to be here any minute now," Miranda gasped, glancing at the clock on the microwave.

"Relax," Kathleen advised. "Just stick to the plan. By the time we get through with him—"

"You don't know Denny," Miranda told her. "Once he sets his mind to something, it's hard to shake him. And he's determined to get me back."

"Look, do you want to go live in Barton for the rest of your life?" Kathleen asked her pointedly.

Miranda shook her head. "No. You know I don't."

"Then you won't. That's all," Kathleen declared.

"But if Denny tells my folks about the band, and the fact that I'm playing in a bar . . ."

"Look, kiddo. I think it's really sweet that you want your parents to approve of what you're doing," Kathleen said sincerely. "But you're eighteen years old, and it's your life. Hell, look at me. I'm making it through school and my folks aren't giving me a dime. They didn't think college was necessary. They just wanted me to get married and have a mess of kids."

"I just don't want them finding out about my music from Denny," Miranda explained. "He'll make it seem all seedy and awful."

"They won't hear anything from Denny," Missy assured her, "because we're not going to let him anywhere near Sally's Pub tonight. We've got it all under control."

"That's what I've been telling her," Kathleen agreed. She turned toward Miranda. "All you have to do is——"

"Stick to the plan," Miranda finished her sentence. But she wasn't so sure.

A few moments later, the doorbell rang. Miranda leaped up from her seat. "That's it. It's him."

"Hey, sit back down," Kathleen told her. "*I'm* greeting him, remember? Phase one of the plan?" She bent down and glanced at her reflection in the window. Then she pulled a black eyeliner pencil from her pocket and deepened the dark circles around her eyes. "Okay, I'm ready," she said, laughing as she left the room and headed for the door.

"Can I help you?" Kathleen asked as she opened the door.

"Um . . . yeah . . . I . . . er . . . is Miranda Lockheart here?"

Miranda had to choke back a laugh as

she listened from the kitchen. Denny sounded so scared. Not at all like the cocky kid he was back in Barton. It was just like Kathleen had predicted.

"Sure, she's in the kitchen. Come on back with me," Kathleen told him. "You must be Donny."

"Denny," he corrected her.

"Oh yeah, the ex." Kathleen's voice had taken on a slightly menacing tone. "Watch your step. You don't want to bump into *Mother.*"

Miranda wished she could see the look on Denny's face as Kathleen pointed Mother out to him. Missy had dressed her specially for Thanksgiving. She was wearing a toy Pilgrim bonnet from the dime store, a loincloth, and Missy's black lace bra. But Miranda was supposed to sit in the kitchen and let Kathleen bring him back to her. That was the plan.

As Miranda heard their footsteps heading through the living room toward the kitchen, she felt her heart pounding. She hadn't seen Denny in so long. She didn't know what she'd feel when their eyes met—or if she'd even feel anything at all.

She didn't have long to find out. A moment later, he was there, standing in her kitchen. Miranda gasped suddenly. She'd forgotten just how tall he was. Or how bright his eyes could shine when he was excited. And he *was* excited to see her.

Surprisingly, she felt a slight thrill at seeing him, too. "Hey, Denny," she said almost shyly, not knowing what to do with her feelings. She'd been so sure she wouldn't· be attracted to him when she saw him. But now, looking at that lone blond curl that had fallen onto his forehead, the one she'd always loved to push back before kissing him . . .

"Hey, Rand," he answered.

"Did you find the place okay?"

He nodded. "I parked outside. Is it, um, safe to leave the car there?"

Kathleen laughed. "Sure, it's safe," she assured him with a suspicious glance. "What exactly are you afraid of?"

"Uh, nothin'," he answered with a gulp. "Just checkin'." He looked around the room. "You got a beer or somethin?" he asked.

"Are you old enough to drink?" Missy

questioned, suddenly getting up from the table and slinking over toward Denny.

"I . . . uh . . . er . . ." Denny wasn't certain how to answer.

"Oh, that's okay." Missy smiled at him as she pulled a bottle from the fridge. "We love jailbait around here." She held out her hand. "I'm Missy," she introduced herself in a voice whose intent could not be mistaken.

Miranda had to choke back a laugh. Missy sure was putting it on thick. And from the look in Denny's eyes, he was completely shell-shocked by the entire experience.

"Uh . . . thanks," he murmured, taking the beer and downing a huge swig. "Miranda, do you think we could spend a little time together? To talk, I mean."

"Sure. We've all been looking forward to talking with you, Denny," Missy said, sidling up to him.

"I think he meant just the two of us," Miranda explained. She turned and smiled at him, feeling instantly—surprisingly—comfortable in his presence. "Sure, Denny."

Something in her tone apparently

concerned Kathleen. She moved closer. "Just remember, you have to leave for class at about six o'clock," she reminded Miranda firmly.

"Do you really have to go to class?" Denny asked her. "I mean, can't you cut just this once?"

"Excuse me?" Kathleen said. "You want Miranda to miss her class? What kind of old friend are you? Don't you want her to succeed here in Austin? Are you here to sabotage her college life? Because if you are—"

"No, hey . . . of course not," Denny said quickly. "I'll wait around here while she's in class and—"

"Oh, that's silly. I can't imagine a strapping young man like you just sitting still." Missy moved closer to Denny and rubbed his arm appreciatively. "A big strong boy like you must work out a lot. Do you run, Denny?"

"Sure, in the woods behind my house, sometimes. I'm pretty fast," he boasted.

"Oh, then you should go for a run while Miranda's in class," Missy suggested. "Austin is so beautiful around sunset. . . ."

"A run? In Austin? At *night?*" Denny sounded petrified.

"Oh, come on," Kathleen said. "You're not afraid, are you? Hell, I run all the time. In fact, why don't you and I take a run together tonight?"

Denny frowned. Now the run was a dare. Anxious not to lose face in front of Miranda, he nodded. "Okay, I'll go for a run. But just a short one."

"Oh, of course," Kathleen assured him, with just the touch of a smirk.

Sally's was packed on Wednesday night. It seemed that a lot of college kids had opted to stay in Austin for the holiday weekend. And they were giving thanks in their own way—mostly by pouring beer down their throats.

"Yo, this is gonna be awesome," Jay shouted over the din of screaming students. "We're gonna rock this place tonight."

"*Plymouth* Rock," Adam joked.

Jay made a face. "Oh, man. That was lame."

Adam looked over at Miranda for support. She usually laughed at his jokes. But she wasn't laughing, or even paying attention. Instead, she was staring distractedly into space. "Hello?" Adam said. "Earth to Miranda."

"Huh? Oh, yeah. Plymouth Rock. Very funny."

"Are you okay?" Adam asked her.

"Yeah. I just have my mind on something else. But don't worry, I'll be okay up there."

"I'm not worried," Adam assured her. "You're always okay behind your drums."

Jay leaped in front of the microphone and grabbed the attention of the beer-swilling crowd. "Hey, guys!" Jay shouted. "Happy Thanksgiving! Are you ready to *Plymouth* Rock this house?"

Miranda and Adam shared a glance. Typical Jay: A joke was lame unless *he* told it!

"Then let's go!" Jay shouted, breaking into the opening riff of "Texas Trilogy."

Miranda joined in, giving a strong downbeat that lead right into Adam's bass riff. Their combined rhythm set the crowd applauding again—it was a signature piece of the Sin-Phony sound, and Sally's regulars loved the combination. Miranda smiled up at Adam as the music filled her mind and her soul, leaving little room for any thoughts about Denny.

But the minute the music stopped, all those thoughts came rushing back. Denny was waiting for her at home. He was going to want to talk. There was no putting this thing off. She was going to have deal with all of her feelings, tonight. It was really confusing. She knew she loved playing at Sally's—being with the guys, creating music that made everyone happy.

And yet . . . there were things she really loved about Denny's world, too. The wide-open spaces of home, riding on horseback through the woods, and the way she'd always felt special in his arms when they were together. She'd had a strange longing for all that, the minute she'd seen him again.

Still, deep in her heart, Miranda knew there was no way those two worlds could ever meet. She'd realized the minute Denny arrived in town that Austin was one place where he'd never fit in. He wasn't a city boy. If she wanted him to be part of her life, she'd have to go back to the small town they'd grown up in. She loved Barton, and she always would consider it home. Still, small-town folks often had small-town ideas about things, and somehow she knew Denny wouldn't want his wife jamming on the drums in a local bar.

No. Miranda could not give up her music and her life here. She was staying in Austin. Denny would have to go back home on his own.

And yet . . . there was something incredibly comforting about the sound of Denny's voice, and the familiarity of his smile.

Her mind was going back and forth like a Ping-Pong ball. It was all so confusing.

"Hey, you okay?" Adam asked as he picked up his bass and walked over to where Miranda was collecting her things.

"Yeah, just a little overwhelmed, I guess."

"Oh . . . ," Adam said slowly. "Your *company* has arrived."

Miranda nodded. "It's hard seeing him again."

"Been there," Adam told her with a knowing nod. "It all sort of comes rushing back as soon as they walk in the room." He sat down and sighed, remembering someone from long ago. Or maybe not so long ago. Miranda couldn't really be sure.

"Your ex . . . ," she began, uncertain of whether Adam really wanted to talk about it.

"Her name was Joni," he continued, his eyes taking on a misty, faraway look. "She was gorgeous—long black hair and the bluest eyes. I'd known her forever, but we didn't get together until sophomore year in high school. After that we were attached at the hip. You'd never see us apart."

Miranda sat there, listening to him, amazed at just how comfortable she felt, despite the intimate nature of their discussion. It certainly was a new experience.

"So you and Joni were together how long?" Miranda asked, suddenly eager to hear more about Adam, although she wasn't altogether sure why.

"Till the summer after graduation.

We'd always planned to come to Lone Star together. We figured we'd get an off-campus apartment, set up house, and be poor, starving students living happily ever after on a steady diet of Ramen noodles and love." He paused for a minute. "At least that's what I had planned. Apparently, Joni had other ideas."

Miranda nodded. So it was this Joni who had broken things off.

"She split for New York City about a week before we were supposed to come up to Austin to look for a place," Adam continued. "I didn't think I'd ever forgive her."

Miranda felt a twinge of guilt. She'd taken off, too, leaving Denny back home in Barton. Of course, they'd never made plans like Adam and Joni had . . . at least not in *her* mind. Still, was it possible that Denny had always just assumed she'd come around to his way of thinking? She'd been angry that Denny had cut her off the way he had. She'd felt as though he'd abandoned her. But maybe he'd felt abandoned too. "Did you ever see her again?" Miranda asked.

"Last summer. She came home a visit. She was very elegant, with a short, sleek hairdo and a tight black minidresses. She talked about cocktail parties, and hanging out in clubs in SoHo. She drank pink Cosmopolitans instead of beer. Man, she was completely changed."

"Did you hate her when you saw her? Or was there a part of you that wanted everything back the way it was?" Miranda was anxious now, trying to see if Adam could answer all the nagging doubts she had about Denny in the back of her mind.

"Hate her? No," Adam said. "But I didn't want to go back to the way things were, either. She wasn't Joni anymore—at least not the Joni I had fallen in love with. And I guess I finally understood where she was coming from. We were on different courses. It wouldn't have been fair to me for her to stay."

"You mean it wouldn't have been fair to *her*," Miranda corrected him.

Adam shook his head. "No. To me. Actually, to either of us. She would have just resented me after a while, and then things would have gotten ugly. We wouldn't have ended up together, but we sure as hell would've wound up bitter. She saw everything clearly way before I did. I should probably thank her. The way she left probably saved both of us years of pain."

Miranda looked at Adam in amazement. She'd never known a guy who was so clear about his emotions, and able to talk about them. Most of the guys she'd ever known thought of feelings as something you cop off a girl. "So how'd you get past it?" she asked him.

Adam shrugged. "I did a whole lot of songwriting." He smiled. "Some of my best work. Depression is great for art."

Miranda smiled back at him. "Well, that's looking at the bright side of things, anyhow."

"Yeah, I guess." Adam stood and picked up his bass. "I've done enough traveling down memory lane for one night. It's your turn now. You've got Denny waiting at home, remember?"

How could she forget?

"You want a lift?" Adam continued.

Miranda shook her head. "I'll take the bus," she assured him.

"That's gonna take forever," he reminded her.

"I know. I don't think I'm in any hurry."

It was nearly midnight when Kathleen and Denny returned to the house from their run. Missy was sitting in the living room in nothing more than a skimpy white nightshirt. She smiled as they came in.

"Get us some water from the fridge," Kathleen ordered Denny as she plopped down on the couch. Denny didn't argue. He was only too happy to get away from her for an instant.

As soon as he was out of earshot, Kathleen whispered to Missy, "Is Miranda back yet?"

"Just got in," Missy told her. "She's in the shower, washing the smell of smoke and beer out of her hair."

"I kept him out as long as I could," Kathleen explained. "I got him good and lost for a while, and then I took him to one of the health bars near the capitol. I figured that would really freak him out. I don't suspect they drink a whole lot of carrot and wheatgrass juice in Barton."

Missy giggled. "It doesn't go too well with barbecue."

"Exactly," Kathleen agreed. "He hated it. He finally insisted on leaving and taking a cab just to make sure we didn't get lost again. I was out of excuses. But I don't think he suspects anything. He kept talking about how Miranda must be out of class by now."

"It's fine," Missy assured her. "Miranda'll be down in a few minutes. I'll take it from here."

"Thank goodness," Kathleen told her. "He's such a drip. No wonder Miranda's so hell-bent on stayin' here. If all the guys in her hometown are like him . . ." She let her voice drift off as she headed up the stairs.

"Where'd Kathleen go?" Denny asked as he returned to the living room with two waters.

"She was a little tired," Missy told him. "She went up to bed."

"Oh, it was a long night," Denny said. "She sure didn't know where she was goin'."

"Mmm. No sense of direction," Missy purred, sidling up close to Denny. "It's always been a problem of hers."

Denny looked down at Missy's skimpy lingerie and cleared his throat. "I'd better go up to Miranda's room. She's probably been wondering where I've been."

Missy listened carefully. She could hear a blow-dryer going in the bathroom. Miranda wasn't quite ready yet. "No!" she exclaimed—a bit too fast. "Um . . . I mean, well, you and I've barely gotten acquainted and I can't bear the thought." She pulled him down on the couch and curled up beside him. "So tell me, what school do you go to?"

"Just the community college near my town," Denny replied, trying to move away from her touch.

"Don't say 'just,'" Missy said. "You're in school—that's what counts. What's your major?"

"Well, I'm going into the family business, so . . ."

"Oh, how exciting," Missy said. She reached over and rubbed his shoulders. "You feel so tense and tight. You need to loosen up."

Denny tried to move away, but she held

on tightly to his arm. "So I'm majoring in . . ."

He never finished his sentence. Miranda appeared on the stairs. "Denny!" she exclaimed.

He leaped up from the couch, getting as far from Missy as possible. "Rand! I can explain. We weren't. I mean, we were just talkin' and . . ."

"Oh, don't worry about Miranda," Missy told him as she headed for the stairs. "She's very understanding. Aren't ya, sugar?"

"Very." As Missy passed by her on the stairs, Miranda gave her a hug. "I owe you one," she whispered in her roommate's ear.

"No sweat. But I'm going to bed," Missy whispered back. "AJ's been waitin' in my room for almost an hour already."

Miranda nodded. AJ was Missy's latest swim-team honey.

Denny yawned and stretched his arms. "What a night. I'm beat. You want to go upstairs?"

Miranda gulped. "Upstairs? To my room? I mean, Denny . . . you and I haven't been . . ."

"Just to talk, Rand," he assured her.

"Denny."

"Come on, Miranda. We can't really talk here," Denny pleaded. "Who knows when one of those two are gonna come down again."

Miranda sighed. He had a point. She slowly rose up from the couch and walked toward the stairs.

"You have some weird roommates," Denny confided as they headed up toward her room.

"I do?"

"Yeah, first Kathleen gets us all turned around and lost in Austin. We wound up clear across town. Then she drags me into this natural-food place where all these health-freak weirdos force me to drink *grass.*" He belched.

Miranda giggled. Obviously, wheatgrass shakes didn't agree with Denny's stomach.

"And then Missy . . . well, what's she doin' parading around dressed like that?"

"You didn't like the way she looked?" Miranda asked him innocently.

"Hell, yeah," Denny said. Then he

stopped himself. "I mean, sure, she looked okay, but . . . it was you I wanted to see, Miranda." He entered the room and sat down on the bed.

Miranda sighed. *Here we go.* "I'm right here, Den."

"I know, and I can hardly believe it," he said excitedly. "I've missed you Rand. Barton's not the same without you."

Somehow Miranda doubted that. Barton was always the same.

"You and I are a good match, Miranda," Denny continued. "You know that. We're not complete unless we're together. I shouldn't have put you on the spot like that at the graduation party. It wasn't fair."

Miranda looked at him kindly. It had taken him months, but he was apologizing to her. That was huge. Denny never apologized to anyone. "It's okay, Denny," she said softly.

"No, it's not," he replied. "I was so embarrassed, and angry. Except I think I was more angry at me than I was at you."

Wow, for Denny, that was pretty deep. Miranda looked into his eyes. A thousand feelings came rushing back all at once. She could recall the smell of his cologne, and the look on his face the first time he told her he loved her. His eyes had been big and hopeful, and she'd felt as though he could see right through her as she told him she felt the same. It had been a magical moment, there in the woods behind his house, with the whole Texas night sky above them.

And now he was here to tell her that he wanted to be a part of her life, and to make her part of his. His eyes were every bit as big now as they'd been then.

"I couldn't call you for the longest time. I had to sort stuff out, y'know. And then, the other night, I realized that I could never be happy without you. And if I can't be happy without you, then it stands to reason that you can't be happy without me. And I really want you to be happy, Miranda. That's why I called."

Miranda sighed. He was wrong. The truth was, despite what he had been feeling back in Barton, *she* had managed to create quite a happy life here in Austin. And she hadn't needed anyone but herself to make that happen. If she was to be truly honest with herself, Denny wasn't part of the picture anymore. She'd moved on. He had to do the same.

She couldn't string him along another minute. It wouldn't be fair. She had to set him free to find the right person. "Denny, I know you and I were happy in high school. And we thought we were in love. But our lives are . . ."

"Shhh . . . ," he whispered. "Don't say it."

"Den, I *have* to tell you."

"Miranda, I know you're still angry about my not calling and all. . . ."

"No Den, I'm not. I understand why you did that. At first I was a little confused. But now I can see that you were right. It was time to break things off. We want different things. You want marriage and a family, and I don't. At least not now."

"You do want those things, too, Rand. You're just being taken in by these weird city folks, but if you were to come home, you'd see that you're not like them."

"They're not weird!" Miranda declared.

"Okay, *different,*" Denny corrected himself.

"Different from who? They're not so different from me."

"Yes, they are," Denny told her.

"No," Miranda insisted. "I'm a lot more like them than I'm like the girl you knew back in high school. That Miranda doesn't exist anymore."

"Yes she does, and I can prove it. Can you honestly say that this doesn't bring it all back?" He moved closer, closer, until his lips were on hers, kissing her passionately, clutching her tightly against him.

The kiss did indeed bring back a flood of memories. But they weren't the type Denny had in mind. Instead, Miranda remembered just how young and immature Denny was. This was the kind of kiss a hungry, anxious teenage boy gave a girl. It lacked any of the patience, gentleness, or sensitivity a real man, someone like Adam, might give.

Whoa. Where did that come from? Miranda pulled away suddenly from Denny, surprised at her own thoughts. *Adam?* She'd never even hugged him, never mind been in this kind of intimate position with him. And yet, he'd been the one who'd raced into her mind. And now that he was there, she knew she'd never be able to get him out. "Denny, please stop," she said quietly, pushing him away.

He stared at her, amazed. "You're kidding, right?"

"This isn't going to work, Denny. You and I both know it."

He turned away and stared at the dresser in the corner of the room. His eyes fell on the pair of drumsticks she'd left lying there.

"Oh, I get it," he said, angrily moving toward the dresser and lifting the sticks. He shoved them in her face. "There's someone else, isn't there?" he demanded. "Some drummer. Well, you'd better watch out for those musical types. They can't be trusted. They're out for just one thing. And a naive girl like you—"

"Naive!" Miranda exploded. "I'm not naive."

"Sure, you are," Denny shouted back. "You don't know a thing about life."

"Well, I know you're wrong about drummers."

"How do you know that?" Denny demanded.

"Because I *am* a drummer. Those are *my* sticks."

Denny chuckled. "Oh, yeah. You're a drummer. A girl drummer. Right." He laughed harder.

"What's so funny about that?"

"Come on, Miranda," Denny said. "Drummer chicks are . . . well, they're wild. And you—"

"You don't know anything about what I'm like when I drum." She frowned. "I knew you wouldn't understand. That's why I asked my roommates to keep you busy while I played that gig tonight."

"That *what*?"

"Gig," Miranda spat out. "There was no night class. I was playing in a bar. And I didn't want you there because I knew you'd just make fun of me. Or, worse yet, try to stop me from doing it. And I won't let anyone put down my drumming. It means too much to me."

But Denny no longer cared about whether she played the drums or not. He was more focused on the wrongs that had been done to him. "You lied to me?" he gasped. "No matter what I may have done,

Miranda, I never lied. I've always been straight with you." He stared at her for a minute, then slammed the drumsticks down on the dresser, shoved his hands into the pockets of his jeans, and turned away. "You know what, you're right: You aren't the same Miranda I used to know."

Miranda sighed. This wasn't easy—for either of them.

"So I guess there's no easy way to tell you this," Denny continued. "But you and I have no future. It's over, Rand." He picked up his bag. "I hope you're not too hurt. But you'll get over me. You'll see."

So now *he* was telling *her* it was over? Miranda frowned, knowing that he'd rewritten the entire history of his visit. He would be sure to tell everyone back home how he'd dumped her, instead of the other way around. For a minute, she considered reminding him that it was *she* who had ended it. But she changed her mind. Why embarrass Denny? Let him save face. She was getting what she wanted: to be completely free of him, once and for all. Despite this whole, miserable evening, she had no desire to hurt him.

In fact, she probably should be grateful to him. If it hadn't been for his kiss, she never might have realized something very important. . . .

Thirteen

If Denny's visit had proven anything, it was that Miranda had made the right decision to come to Austin. In fact, many of the decisions she'd made were the right ones . . . for her, anyway. She'd thought them out, made her own choices, and managed to carve out a life for herself that she was proud of. She guessed that was what being an adult was about: making your own decisions.

It was also about taking ownership of those decisions, and not being afraid that others might not approve. Which was exactly what she was thinking as she dialed her home number Thursday morning.

"Howdy, sugar," her mother greeted her. "Happy Thanksgiving."

"Happy Thanksgiving, Mom. How're things back home?"

"Not the same without you," Mrs. Lockheart admitted. "But we're hangin' in there." She paused for a minute and cleared her throat slightly. "I heard you were gettin' company this weekend."

"Denny," Miranda confirmed. "He came for a few hours yesterday. But he's gone now."

"Oh." Her mom sounded noncommittal, waiting to hear how Miranda felt about things.

"We're just in two different places now," Miranda told her. "So we ended things. I think it's best."

"So do I," her mother agreed. "He's not for you, sugar. He'll never be more than his daddy's puppet. Whereas my little girl's got a mind of her own."

If she only knew.

"Well, Mom, the thing is, that's kinda what I've called you about. You're probably going to hear about this from Denny, so I thought I should tell you first."

There was a slightly audible gasp from the other end of the line. "Sure. Go ahead, sugar. You know you can tell me anything."

"Well, the thing is, Mom, I've sort of taken up playing the drums."

There was dead silence on the phone. Then Miranda's mom started laughing.

"I'm serious, Mom. I'm a drummer. In a band. We play here in a place called Sally's Pub every week."

Mrs. Lockheart caught her breath. "I'm sorry, honey. I wasn't laughing at you. I was just so relieved. You made it sound like Denny was going to tell me something awful."

"Then you don't mind?"

"Mind? Why would I mind you taking up an instrument? I sent you to college to learn new things."

Wow. Miranda was totally blown away. She hadn't expected her mom to take it this way. She sounded very un-mom-like. Kinda cool, even.

"Now this bar—you're not drinking while you're there, are you? Because you're underage, you know."

Miranda smiled. There, now she sounded like her mom again. "No. I'm not drinking."

"And the other kids in the band? They're nice? Not drug addicts or anything?"

"No, Mom. No drugs. I swear."

"Well, good. I'm glad you have a new hobby, then," Mrs. Lockheart said, obviously relieved.

"It's more than a hobby, Mom. It's a passion. I'm thinking of being a music major at school. I want this to be my life."

"Whoa, slow down, honey," Miranda's mom warned. "Playing the drums is one thing, but making them your career is a horse of another color. I mean, be *logical,* Miranda. What kind of life is that? It's so unsure. A musician. Most of them starve."

"I'm not going to starve, Mom."

"You're so young. You don't know how hard life can be. Now with a good profession, you can make things a lot easier for yourself."

Miranda sighed. "This is exactly why I didn't want to say anything to you and Dad about this. I knew you'd be against it."

"I'm not against your taking music classes, honey, I swear," her mom assured her. "But this music major thing . . . well, have you even looked into it? I'm sure you have to take more than just drumming classes. You probably have to know how to read music. You never learned how to do that."

"Oh." Miranda's voice grew small. She hadn't considered the possibility that she didn't have the skills required for a music major. The disappointment soaked right through her. She could barely speak.

"Look, we don't need to plan your whole life right now, do we?" her mother asked gently, obviously sensing the disappointment in her daughter's voice. "We can talk more when you're home for Christmas. In the meantime, I think you should be very proud of yourself. It's not everyone who can pick up an instrument and be playing in public so soon. You must be really talented. I wish I could hear you."

"I do, too, Mom. It would be so great if you could come to one of our gigs."

"Maybe we'll drive up one time," her

mother assured her. "And Miranda . . ."

"What?"

"Don't ever be afraid to tell me something, okay? I may not always agree with you, but I do want to know what you're up to."

"Okay, Mom. I promise."

"And bring home that class catalog when you come for Christmas," Mrs. Lockheart continued. "Maybe we can find a music class for nonmajors that you can take next semester. That would be a good way to see if this is what you really want."

Miranda and her mom spoke for a few more minutes, then Mrs. Lockheart passed the phone around to Miranda's dad, her aunt Marcy, three of her cousins, and even the dog. After exchanging a few barks with Sparky, Miranda finally hung up the phone. *There.* That hadn't gone so badly. Her mom had been pretty okay about the whole drum thing. At least as long as it wasn't her major.

But her mother was in for a battle on that one. Miranda didn't shy away from difficult situations—at least not anymore.

Miranda sat there for a moment, thinking

about what her family was doing now. Her mom was most likely dressing the turkey while her dad was vegging out on the couch, watching a football game and drinking a few beers. No doubt her cousins were arguing over which two of them could break the wishbone after the meal. She sighed heavily. Missing Thanksgiving at home was harder than she'd thought.

But then she remembered what she had to look forward to in Austin: seeing Adam! Now *that* was something to give thanks for.

Miranda opened her closet and pulled out a new pair of jeans and a pale blue button-down cotton shirt that she knew brought out her eyes. She brushed her long blond hair until it shone like the sun, and then put on her cowboy hat. Finally, she slipped into her Frye boots, zipped up a fleece sweatshirt, and headed for the door.

As she walked toward the bus stop, Miranda thought about the way her feelings for Adam had snuck into her subconscious without her even knowing it. Last night with Denny wasn't even the first time the thought of him had stopped her from making out with a guy. There had been that night at the party, when the very thought of him was all it had taken to convince her she wasn't ready to sleep with Paul. And she had barely even spoken to him. Still, there must have been some attraction that had made her think of him in a moment like that. She took that as proof that they were meant to be. *Now she just had to convince Adam of that.*

Miranda tried to imagine how he might react when she told him what she was thinking. Of course, she was prepared for him to be surprised. He probably had no idea how Miranda really felt about him. Why would he? Up until last night, Miranda herself had no clue. But now that she knew, she couldn't wait to see him.

Rikyu was surprisingly crowded on Thanksgiving afternoon. Apparently a lot of the Austin college crowd had opted for raw fish over turkey this Thanksgiving.

"Can I help you?" a beautiful Japanese woman in a silk kimono greeted her.

"I'm meeting a crowd of friends here," Miranda explained, her eyes darting around the restaurant until they landed on a rowdy table near the back. "Oh, there they are."

"I believe they've started without you."

"That's okay," Miranda assured the hostess. As she began walking back toward the group, a feeling of nervousness came over her. Things were going to change today, she knew it. If Adam felt the way she did (and, boy, she really hoped he did!), then the dynamics of Sin-Phony were going to change too. Permanently. And she didn't know how any of them were going to deal with that. Okay . . . well, she, didn't know how Jay, she and Adam would deal. Bobby's reaction was pretty easy to predict: He'd be mad at the "chick" for changing things.

"Miranda!" Kathleen shouted out as soon as her roommate came into view. "What're you doin' here?"

"I'm here for Thanksgiving dinner," she answered.

All eyes turned toward Miranda. It was only then that she realized there were a few different faces in the group. Besides the band members and Kathleen, three other girls were seated at the table. They looked vaguely familiar; Miranda thought she'd seen them at a few of the Sally's Pub shows, but she couldn't be sure.

"Where's Denny?" Kathleen asked.

"He went home," Miranda replied. "For good." She stared right into Adam's kind brown eyes as she said that last part, making sure he understood.

"Well, pull up a chair," Jay said with a smile, motioning toward the head of the table, a spot that would put her about as far from Adam as possible. Not that Miranda could have gotten a seat beside him, anyway. He was flanked on either side by a girl.

Miranda looked down at Jay's plate. "What is that?" she asked, staring at the odd arrangement of raw fish.

"Thanksgiving special," Jay explained. He pointed to the gray fish. "That's mackerel. It's kind of the color of turkey. And that red fish, the tuna, is supposed to represent the cranberry sauce. I guess the orangey salmon is supposed to be like the yams."

Miranda made a face. Somehow, raw fish, no matter what the colors, just couldn't pull it off as a Thanksgiving feast.

"Hey, you're the drummer, aren't you?" one of the girls, a small brunette in quite possibly the tightest tank top Miranda had ever seen, shouted from across the table.

"Yes," Miranda answered.

"That's so cool," the girl continued. "I never saw a girl drummer before."

"Neither had I," Bobby told her, "till I met Miranda here."

"Miranda, that's a pretty name," squealed another of the girls, this one a bit taller, with long red curls, but also wearing impossibly tight clothing.

"Not as pretty as yours," Bobby told her.

"Do you even remember my name?" she asked him teasingly.

"Sure. It's Danielle."

The girl rolled her eyes and hit him with her napkin. "Daniel*la*," she corrected him.

"Hey, I was close." Bobby shrugged. "But don't worry, honey. I kept one promise. I still respected you in the morning."

Obviously she was Bobby's latest conquest. A wave of worry suddenly washed over Miranda. If Bobby and this Daniella person had been together last night, then what about the other two girls? What if one of them had been with Adam? Which one might it have been? She'd never seen Adam with any girl before. She didn't know his type at all.

"I'm Elise," the small brunette in the tank top introduced herself, interrupting the sudden burst of panic in Miranda's head. Elise pointed to her friend, a strawberry blonde with blue eyes who, despite the November chill in the air, had chosen to wear a halter top to Thanksgiving dinner. "And this is Billie Jane."

"I thought you were the greatest," Billie Jane told Miranda. "I love this band. They're the best Sally's has had in a long time."

"Thanks," Miranda replied. "But Adam deserves a lot of the credit. He and I work together. We're the rhythm section."

"My boy here's got the rhythm method down, don't you, Adam?" Bobby agreed, reaching past Daniella to pat him on the back.

Adam laughed but said nothing.

Miranda frowned. He was being incredibly quiet. *Suspiciously* quiet.

The girls, however, weren't at all quiet. They giggled conspiratorially at Bobby's little double entendre.

"So you sent Denny packing," Kathleen said, interrupting the hideous cackling laughter.

"I think he realized I wasn't going home," Miranda told her. "And he definitely didn't like things in Austin."

"I'll bet," Kathleen said, laughing.

"Did you bring him to the gig?" Daniella asked.

"Are you saying our music would drive a boy out of town?" Bobby teased her.

"No," Daniella replied quickly. "I was just wondering if I might've seen him last night."

"I thought you only had eyes for me," Bobby said.

"Oh, you know that's true," Daniella said, pressing up against him.

"No, Denny didn't come to the show," Miranda told her. "He and I are from a small town. People from there are not always open to the idea of girl drummers."

"Oh, you're a small-town girl." Elise giggled. "I hear they're the wildest."

"Miranda's definitely wild behind the drums," Jay agreed. "I think we have the hottest rhythm section in town."

"Thanks, dude," Adam said, finally opening his mouth to speak. He smiled at Miranda. "It is a great partnership."

Miranda grinned back, relieved that he'd finally taken some notice of her.

"You and Miranda are *partners?*" Elise asked him. There was more than a twinge of disappointment in her voice.

"Sure," Adam said, turning toward Miranda and giving her another one of his broad, genuine smiles. She nearly melted under his gaze, but he didn't seem to notice. Instead, he switched his glance to Elise. "When you work in a band, it's like being part of a team. And Miranda here's taught us all a little bit about teamwork. She's also a kick-ass ballplayer. You should see her shootin' hoops."

"You're into basketball, too?" Billie Jane asked, surprised.

"Hell, yeah," Jay said. "It's a prerequisite for being in Sin-Phony. You gotta shoot hoops. It's the best way to unwind after a jam session."

"Well, not the *best* way," Bobby disagreed, reaching down and pinching Daniella playfully on the rear end.

"Yeah, but hoops are a close second," Adam told him. "Don't you think so, Rand?"

"Sure," Miranda said quietly.

Suddenly, Adam raised his soda glass. "To Miranda," he toasted her. "We're all glad to have her on the team."

"To Miranda," the others agreed, raising their glasses.

Miranda tried hard to smile graciously. But it was tough. Adam had just made it clear that he thought of her as one of the guys. A band member. His partner in the rhythm section. A great hoops player. *Damn.* He didn't share her feelings at all.

"You want to order something?" A waitress appeared at Miranda's side with her pad and pencil in hand.

"No thanks," Miranda replied wearily. "Suddenly, I'm not very hungry."

Fourteen

"He treated me like one of the guys. He even asked if I wanted to shoot hoops with him and Bobby in the college gym tonight," Miranda moaned as she sat on Missy's bed Thanksgiving night, drowning her sorrows in a bowl of popcorn. She'd been confiding in Missy all evening. Her roommate had proven to be an awfully good listener.

"Well, of course, he did, honey," Missy told her honestly. "Just look at you."

"What're you talking about?" Miranda asked, surprised.

"I'm talking about what you're wearing. Those jeans and that shirt. My cousin

Harold has the same outfit. He wears it whenever he goes to the movies."

"Real funny." Miranda scowled. "I'm not in the mood for jokes."

"Who's joking? The truth is, if you want Adam to think of you as a woman, you've got to *dress* like a woman. I mean, that outfit doesn't exactly scream 'Look at me, I'm a sexy babe who's really into you,' does it?"

Miranda looked at the jeans and button-down shirt she had on. It *was* kind of manly compared with what Billie Jane, Elise, and Daniella had been wearing. Adam had seemed to notice that *they* were girls.

"And hell, you look good today compared with the way you are when you come home from a night of rehearsal and basketball."

Miranda scowled. Missy was taking this tough-love thing a bit too far.

"You've got to change Adam's perception of you." Missy continued. "You've been dressing to rope a cow. It's time to start dressing to rope in a man."

Miranda thought about the jeans, tank tops, sweatshirts, and blouses hanging in her closet. There wasn't anything in there that could pass for the kind of outfit Missy was talking about.

It was as if her roommate could read her mind. "I have an idea," Missy exclaimed suddenly. "Let's go shopping tomorrow! It's Black Friday—you know: the day after Thanksgiving. Everybody's having sales. It'll be so much fun."

Miranda's cell phone rang early Friday morning. She rolled over, grabbed it from the cinder-block nightstand beside her bed, and pushed the On button. "Hello," she mumbled in a groggy voice.

"Did I wake you?"

Miranda shot up in bed at the sound of Adam's voice. It made her feel warm all over—even warmer than the wool blanket she was currently wrapped in. "No . . . I . . ."

"Yes, I did," Adam continued. "I'm sorry."

"It's okay. I had to get up, anyhow."

"Oh, you have plans?" Adam asked. He sounded disappointed. "I was hoping you were free today."

Her heart began to pound wildly. He *had* noticed her. He wanted to spend the day with her. Missy had been totally wrong. She didn't need to change her look to attract Adam after all. "What did you have in mind?" she wondered, adding just a subtle tinge of flirtatiousness to her voice.

But Adam seemed totally clueless to any flirting. "Well, no offense. I mean, I think I'm as much at fault as you. But our playing was slightly out of sync on Wednesday night. I figured we should go down to the studio and work on our part of a few of the songs before we play at Sally's again on Wednesday."

Miranda could literally feel the wind being knocked out of her. *Band business.* That's what this was all about. The disappointment was overwhelming.

For a moment, she thought about agreeing to meet him at the studio. After all, being around Adam was what she really wanted, wasn't it? She should take it however she could get it.

"Then, after we could go to the gym and shoot hoops with the other guys or something," Adam continued.

The other *guys.* Meaning Jay and Bobby. That settled it. Miranda didn't want to be around Adam if he was going to think about her as one of the guys. In the end, shopping with Missy would be a better way to go about moving her relationship with Adam to the next level. "No, I'm sorry. I really can't," she told him. "I promised Missy I'd go shopping with her today."

"Shopping? You?" Adam sounded genuinely surprised.

"Yeah," Miranda replied.

"You'd rather shop with Missy than jam on the drums?"

"What? A girl can't shop on the biggest sale day of the year?" Miranda asked indignantly.

"Yeah, sure she can. I mean *you* can," Adam replied, clearly flustered. "I just didn't think you were the kind of . . . I mean . . . I didn't know you like to shop."

She didn't. Not really. In fact, she hadn't bought anything but school supplies, textbooks, and drumsticks since she'd been in Austin. But things were going to change. Right now. *They had to.*

"There's a lot you don't know about me, Adam," she replied.

"What do you mean you don't wear a bra?" Missy was incredulous, not to mention incredibly loud, as she and Miranda walked into a lingerie store in the Northcross Mall.

"It's not like I have all that much to fill one," Miranda whispered to her.

"Oh, on the contrary, my dear. With the right lift, you'll have plenty. Besides, you know what they say: 'More than a handful's a waste'!" Missy picked up a black lacy underwire number and examined it. "This'll work. Wait until you see how this thing lifts and separates."

Missy ushered Miranda into a little room and waited outside while she tried on the bra. Miranda did as she was told, fastening the contraption behind her and slipping on the straps. Then she looked at herself in the mirror. Missy wasn't kidding. The bra *did* give her a lift. She actually had cleavage!

Still, the bra wasn't completely comfortable. She hated the feeling of the straps over her shoulders, and she knew that after a while that wire was going to cut into her. But she could take it for a few hours— especially if it would make Adam notice that she was a girl.

"It fits," Miranda shouted from the dressing room.

"Good!" Missy exclaimed. "I'll go get two more—one in white, and one in nude. And a couple of thongs. They're on an amazing sale. They'll fit right into your budget."

Miranda frowned. Some budget. In order to buy clothes today, she'd be living on peanut butter and jelly until she went home for Christmas.

As the girls left the store, they walked by the ice-skating rink in the middle of the mall. Miranda was instantly drawn to the rink. She'd never seen one right in the middle of a shopping mall before. And the kids skating around the ice looked they were having so much fun—which was a lot more than Miranda could say at the moment.

"Oh no," Missy warned, reading Miranda's mind. "We've still got plenty of work to do. For starters, we've got to get you a couple of skirts."

"Oh, no. That's where I draw the line. I can't drum in skirts."

"But Miranda, skirts are really in, and they're so sexy. You have amazing legs. You should show them off. If I had long legs like yours, I'd wear nothing *but* short skirts. . . ."

Miranda shook her head. "No way."

"Fine," Missy harrumphed, dragging Miranda into a funky clothing store near the food court. "We'll get you some new pants—maybe ones that lace up on the side; or really low-slung ones."

"I hate those," Miranda groaned. "Your underwear sticks out."

"That's why we got you the thongs," Missy reminded her.

"Great, so instead of underwear, my whole butt will stick out."

"It's called rear cleavage," Missy corrected her. "And it's very in these days. *Adam* will love it. Trust me. When it comes to what guys want, I'm the expert."

Miranda sighed. It was hard to argue with that.

"I can't breathe in these jeans," Miranda groaned as she walked into Missy's room on the Sunday afternoon after the shopping spree. She was getting ready to go to a Sin-Phony rehearsal. Her first since she had purchased her new wardrobe.

"Whoa, check you out," Missy exclaimed. "You look amazing."

"You really think so?" Miranda asked, unsure.

"Oh, yeah. Those highlights we put in your hair really make it all come together."

Miranda glanced in the full-length mirror in the wall. Missy had put a few streaks of almost white-blond into Miranda's naturally wheat-colored hair. She had to admit it did light up her face. She liked the highlights. Which was more than she could say about the rest of the outfit. Everything she was wearing seemed too small, and extremely uncomfortable. Especially that thong. It felt like a piece of floss stuck between her cheeks.

"You'd better get goin'," Missy told her. "The boys are waitin'. Now, when you get back, I want to hear all the juicy details."

Miranda was a little late getting to practice. Already, the three guys were busy setting up their amps and tuning their instruments. But they stopped suddenly when Miranda walked into the room.

"Whoa!" Bobby exclaimed. He couldn't take his eyes off of her. "Check you out!" He let out a whistle that was usually reserved for one of the girls in the audience.

Jay seemed equally amazed. "Wow," he muttered under his breath. "Hot damn."

Miranda was pleased with their reaction. They had definitely noticed her. But she hadn't heard from the most important member of the band yet. He was busy staring at her. Miranda felt as though she were going to melt under his gaze. Her cheeks began to burn. She bit her lip and waited for some comment from Adam.

Finally he spoke. "What'd you do to your hair?"

Miranda shot him a coquettish smile— the kind she'd seen Missy give a million times. "I added a few highlights. Do you like it? It's supposed to make it look sun-kissed."

"*Kissed,* huh?" Bobby butted in. "So that's it. Miranda's got a guy."

"A lucky guy," Jay agreed, walking

behind her to admire her rear end.

Miranda was growing uncomfortable. Jay and Bobby were looking at her like she was a piece of meat. Adam didn't seem to be looking at her at all. This was working out all wrong.

"No. I don't have a new guy. Just some new clothes," she said, taking a seat behind the drums.

"Are you okay?" Adam asked her, suddenly sounding concerned.

"Sure. Why?" Miranda replied.

"I don't know. You have a funny look on your face. Like you have a stomachache or something."

Miranda shook her head. "No. I'm fine." But she really wasn't. The jeans were even tighter when she sat down. She could barely breathe. She just hoped they wouldn't split when she started drumming.

"Okay," Adam said, focusing his attention on tuning his bass.

"Hey, you still haven't told me if you like my hair this way," Miranda reminded him, trying to bring his attention back to the new her.

Adam shrugged. "What do I know

about hair?" he asked her. "I haven't cut mine in months."

"Well, *I* know something," Jay interrupted. "We have less than an hour left in studio time. So we'd better get jammin'. Let's start with the new tune, 'Tunnel Vision.' I think the rhythm was a little off on that last time."

Adam shot Miranda a look that said, *I told you so.* She turned away from his glance. That wasn't the kind of look she'd been hoping for at all.

The rehearsal actually went pretty well, though, all things considered. The denim on the jeans loosened a bit, and the underwire in her push-up bra didn't start to cut into her until they were almost through. Still, by the time they reached the end of their scheduled time in the studio, Miranda was ready to whip off the whole outfit and crawl into a nice pair of baggy sweats and a T-shirt.

And the suffering hadn't even been worth it. Adam split, right after rehearsal, begging off from their usual beer-and-basketball relaxation routine to study for a physics test.

"Physics, my butt," Bobby groaned as

Adam headed out the door. "More like *physical*."

"What, Adam's got a girl?" Jay said. "Hot damn. It's about time."

Miranda gasped slightly, almost audibly. Luckily, the guys didn't seem to notice.

"That's my guess," Bobby replied. "Ever since that Wednesday night gig, he keeps saying he's got plans anytime I try to get him to come along with me to a club or somethin'. I figure he hooked up with one of the chicks who were at the gig that night."

Miranda scowled as she packed up her drumsticks.

"Nah," Jay replied. "They're not his type."

"Really?" Bobby asked curiously. "What is his type?

Jay shrugged. "I have no idea. I've never met anyone he's dated. But I don't think two trampy groupies are exactly what Adam's into."

Miranda could only hope he was right.

Missy was waiting in the kitchen when Miranda arrived home Sunday night.

"You're late," she said excitedly. "I hope that means you were with Adam."

"No," Miranda replied ruefully. "I spent the night with my sociology paper in the library."

"Oh."

"He didn't even notice my clothes," Miranda groaned.

"Oh, come on, he must have noticed. You look so hot," Missy assured her.

"I'm telling you, he was all business. He played his bass and split."

"He didn't even talk to you?"

"Not about anything but music," Miranda told her. "Usually he jokes around with me and stuff. But tonight . . . he didn't even offer me a lift home or anything."

"Then he definitely noticed you," Missy told her. "He's just in shock. It's so obvious what caused his change in behavior. His little buddy has suddenly turned into a hottie, and he doesn't know how to handle it."

That made sense. "I guess . . . ," Miranda said slowly.

"No. That's what it is. He's just digesting

all the changes. You probably knocked him over like a ton of bricks. Wait until your next rehearsal . . . when is it?"

"Tuesday."

"Tuesday," Missy repeated. "He's gonna be all over you."

When Miranda arrived at the studio on Tuesday night, Adam was already there. She looked around for Jay and Bobby, but they weren't there. It was just she and Adam. The thought of it made her nervous, and excited. It was a strange feeling. She was anticipating something, but she didn't know what. "Hi there," she said as she walked into the room, trying desperately to sound casual.

"Hey."

"You're here early."

Adam shrugged. "I was already in the neighborhood, and I wanted to finish up the last verse of a new song I'm writing." He glanced up, and for the first time got a look at Miranda in her latest outfit: a pair of tight black slacks and a skimpy silver cami. Missy had done her makeup, too, adding some silver body glitter to her arms and shoulders just to catch the light . . . and Adam's eye.

But it wasn't the glitter that caught his attention. It was the black heels Miranda was wearing—she'd borrowed them from Missy. "How're you going to play in those?" he asked her.

Miranda sighed. The music. It was all he was thinking about. "I'm going to take them off and play in my bare feet."

"Why didn't you just wear your sneaks?"

"They didn't match my outfit," Miranda told him, in a desperate attempt to make him notice how sexy she was dressed.

It worked. For the first time, Adam seemed to see Miranda's new clothes. "Oh," he replied. He studied her glittery new look for a moment and then asked, "You going anywhere after rehearsal?"

Was he asking her out? This could be it. The moment that everything changed. "I don't have any plans," Miranda replied, her voice shaking ever so slightly.

Adam shifted his weight back and forth nervously. "You mean you dressed like that just to jam?" he asked incredulously.

Before Miranda could answer him, Jay and Bobby came racing into the room. "Hot damn!" Bobby shouted excitedly. "Hot damn!"

"Hot damn what?" Adam said, looking away from Miranda.

"You won't believe it! This is huge," Bobby continued.

"What's huge, man?" Adam asked.

"We're in. We're in."

"In where?" Adam begged.

"The Austin Jam, that's where," Jay shouted.

Adam brushed a strand of his long brown hair from his eyes. "That *is* huge."

"What's the Austin Jam?" Miranda asked.

Jay seemed to notice her for the first time. "Whoa. Check you out. What'd you do, raid Missy's closet?"

Miranda blushed.

"Missy. That's who you remind me of," Adam said finally. "I've been trying to figure it out."

"Are you going fishing for swim team members, too?" Bobby asked, laughing.

"No," Miranda insisted. "I just bought some new clothes. That's all. Anyway, what's the Austin Jam?" she asked again, changing the subject.

"It's a showcase," Adam explained to her. "There's about fifteen or so bands that play. It goes on all night, from eight P.M. till eight in the morning." He turned to Jay. "What spot did we get?"

"Four A.M.," Jay said.

"Oh well, that's not too bad," Adam said.

"Yeah, at least we're not the opening act."

"We'll have the diehards in the audience. That's cool," Jay said. "And they'll be drunk enough by then to really want to hear us."

"Or so drunk, they're throwing up," Adam joked.

Miranda made a face.

"Oh, I forgot, there's a girl in the room," Adam said, and bowed low. "My apologies, m'lady."

Miranda smiled, pleased that he'd finally noticed. But a moment later, he seemed to have forgotten. "We need to get practicing, then," he said, picking up his bass. "The Austin Jam's usually the last week in January."

"Yeah, we'd better get on it. We need to be really smokin' that night. This could mean a whole new group of gigs for us," Bobby agreed.

"A step up from Sally's," Jay suggested.

Miranda got caught up in their enthusiasm. She whipped off her heels and picked up her sticks. She began tapping out a beat on her drums. Adam picked up her rhythm and began to pluck his bass along with her. A few moments later, Jay and Bobby joined in, jammin' powerfully through the free-form tune.

They were all so lost in the moment, that they were shocked when the manager of the studios poked his head in the room to tell them their practice time was up.

It may have been time to stop playing, but none of them was ready to give up the high they'd just experienced. They wanted to celebrate in their own unique way. There was still plenty of steam to burn off.

"You guys want to head over to the Lone Star College gym and shoot a few?" Bobby suggested.

"How about a beer instead?" Miranda suggested, smiling up at Adam.

Adam shook his head. "Not me. I'm busted."

"Me too," Jay agreed. "Christmas presents, you know."

"I'll go if you're buyin', Miranda," Bobby said.

No way *that* was happening. She'd spent all her cash on the new clothes she'd bought with Missy. "Sorry," she told Bobby. "No can do."

"Then hoops it is," Jay said, grabbing his guitar. "How about two on two."

Bobby looked over at Miranda. "That outfit is definitely not for sports—at least not basketball," he teased.

Miranda blushed.

"I guess the three of us'll have to just do some shooting, then," Jay said.

"Well, maybe we can get into a pickup game," Adam suggested.

"Yeah, okay," Bobby agreed as he headed toward the door.

"You cool with this, Rand?" Jay asked her.

"Yeah sure, have fun," she said. Then she glanced at Adam, hoping he'd offer to give her a lift or something. But no such luck. "See you at the gig," he told her.

Miranda sighed as the guys left without her. Sooner or later, Adam would recognize her as the perfect woman for him. Miranda was sure of it. She just wished it wasn't taking him so damn long to figure it out.

Fifteen

"What *are* you wearing?" Kathleen asked as Miranda walked into Sally's Pub on Wednesday evening, just in time for the band's soundcheck.

Miranda looked down at her silky red halter and short denim cut-offs. "What's wrong with it?" she replied.

"You just don't look like you," Kathleen continued. "I mean, could those shorts *be* any smaller?"

"They're comfortable," Miranda lied. "Good to drum in."

"They're good for something," Kathleen murmured. "But I'm not so sure it's drumming. So who is he?"

"Who's who?"

"The guy you've put on this outfit for," Kathleen demanded. "Come on, spill it."

For a brief moment Miranda thought about telling Kathleen how she felt about Adam. But she changed her mind. It was better that only she and Missy knew for now. Telling all her friends would be *so* high school. "It's nobody."

"All right, don't tell me. But you should know that changing your clothes isn't the way to get a guy to like you. He should get to like the real you. The one *inside.* What's on the outside shouldn't matter."

Miranda choked back a laugh at the irony of that comment. At the moment, Miss Inner-Loveliness was wearing a black leather skirt, torn fishnet stockings, big black boots, and a vintage Billy Idol T-shirt. "Look, I gotta go set up the drums," Miranda said finally. "I'll see you after the set."

"Cool. I'm going to go see if Jay needs anything."

Miranda nodded and headed for the stage. A few minutes later, Adam and

Bobby came up behind her, setting up their instruments as well.

"Nice," Bobby said as he glanced appreciatively at Miranda's outfit. "That'll bring in some paying customers."

"They're here to listen to the music," Adam reminded him. "Not ogle the drummer."

"Hey, whatever brings 'em in. Remember, we get a piece of the door. And I for one could use the cash."

Adam turned away from the two of them and began tuning his bass. Miranda hit the drums a few times, checking for sound, then bent over to pick up her extra sticks. As she bent down, Adam got a clear view of her scantily clad rear end—complete with the Y-shaped straps of her thong peering out over the edge of her shorts.

"Oops," Miranda said, embarrassed. She really wasn't comfortable with this whole dress-for-success-with-Adam plan. But she was determined to stick with it. So she stood up and flashed Adam as confident a smile as she could muster. "I guess that's not my best angle," she teased him play-

fully, seeing that his face had turned beet-red. *Well, at least he noticed.*

Before Adam could reply, Jay leaped onto the stage, his guitar in hand. "Sally wants us to get started a few minutes early tonight, because the crowd's gettin' rowdy. So let me just plug in my ax and Miranda, you give us the count."

"Okay," she agreed, taking her seat behind her drum set and getting ready to play.

Bobby wasn't kidding about Miranda's new look causing a stir among the male clientele at Sally's. Sure enough, plenty of guys in the audience were taking notice of Miranda as she jammed with Adam, Bobby, and Jay. Unfortunately, the one guy she *wanted* to pay her a little mind, was completely ignoring her. In fact, as soon as Sin-Phony finished their set, Adam walked off the stage and joined Bobby in a crowd of scantily dressed well-wishers.

I don't get it. He'll talk to them, but not to me? Those girls weren't wearing anything any more revealing than Miranda's outfit, and they sure weren't as pretty. Yet Adam seemed to notice them. Big-time. At the moment, he had his arm around one tall, buxom brunette in a silver and black tube top and black leather pants. She was whispering something into his ear that made him smile.

It was the smile that killed her. She loved Adam's smile. And the fact that it was aimed at someone other than her was too much for Miranda to handle.

"Hey, little drummer girl, can I buy you a drink?" a tall, muscular guy with short brown hair that had been dyed blond at the tips snuck up behind Miranda.

She whipped around suddenly, getting a good look into his small green eyes. Ordinarily, she would have told him no thank you and left, but tonight she was in a different state of mind. What was good for the guys was good for her as well. Why shouldn't she let this guy buy her a drink? "Sure," she told him. "How about a shooter?"

"Well, all right," the guy with the green eyes agreed. "I told my buddies you were a real party girl."

"You were right," Miranda smiled as she followed him over to the bar.

"I'm Harris," Mr. Green Eyes introduced himself. He pointed to his two friends. "And this is Mark and JT."

"Howdy," Miranda said, flashing them the same sort of smile Adam had given the girl in the tube top.

"We'll have a shooter over here for the lady," Harris told a passing waitress.

Instantly the waitress stopped in front of them and placed a shot glass on the bar. She pulled a cap gun from her belt and set off one of the caps. *Bang!*

The loud noise got the attention of everyone in the bar—including Adam. Miranda could feel his eyes on her as the waitress poured the liquor into the shot-glass.

Miranda picked up the glass and put it to her lips. Suddenly she heard a familiar voice ringing out through the crowd.

"Miranda, Miranda, Miranda!"

It was Bobby, cheering her on. His deep voice was soon joined by Jay's. "Miranda. Miranda. Miranda."

She turned to them, held the shot glass up where they could see it, and then downed the booze in one gulp. *Oh, man.*

That burned going down. But it was worth it. Adam had seen her drink too. Now he could tell that she was every bit the same party girl as the women he was hanging out with on the other side of the bar.

"How about *I* buy you one, now?" JT suggested.

"Come on, I brought her over here," Harris argued. "Miranda's with me."

"No way. Let the lady choose," JT countered. "Miranda?"

"Well, I guess one more wouldn't hurt," Miranda agreed. "If y'all will have one, too."

"Sure, we'll all have one," Mark assured her. He turned to the waitress. "Set 'em up, honey."

The waitress did as she was asked, setting up three additional shot glasses and raising her cap gun in the air—this time letting out four shots, one for each customer. Once again, all eyes turned toward Miranda.

While the first drink had burned going down, Miranda noticed that the second shooter was smoother—maybe because her throat had already been burned, or because she was already feeling the numbing effect of the liquor. Either way, she liked this second drink a whole lot more. "Woohoo!" she exclaimed. "That was good."

"So how long you been playing drums?" Harris asked Miranda.

"Not long," she told him honestly. "A few months, maybe."

"Wow, really?" he replied. "The way you were going at it up there, I thought you'd been playing all your life."

Miranda shook her head. "Nope. I guess I'm just a natural."

The guys all smiled, and then began to talk loudly among themselves, each bragging a bit for her benefit. It turned out JT was supposedly a kick-ass saxophone player in his high school marching band, while Mark had taught himself to play "Chopsticks" on the piano by the time he was five.

Miranda was barely listening to their chatter. Rather, she was focusing on the warm feeling that had rushed over her body. Probably the shooter taking effect, she figured.

"Hey, why are you still standing?"

Harris asked her. "You're not just gonna drink and run, are you, Miranda?"

"Me? No. Of course not," Miranda replied with a smile. She moved to sit on a bar stool beside him, but missed the seat. *Boom.* She crashed down onto the floor. "Oops . . . I missed. Those shooters sure do sneak up on ya, don't they?" she joked, trying to remain as graceful as possible while Harris yanked her up by the elbow.

"Oh yeah, that's part of their charm," JT told her. "You never see it comin'."

"They're fun, though," Miranda replied.

"You know, I play a little guitar," Harris interrupted. Apparently, he felt it was his turn to boast about his musical prowess.

"Really?" she replied, feigning interest.

"Uh-huh. Maybe you'd like to come back to my place and make some music?" He moved closer to her, his breath hot on her neck.

Miranda gulped. She was lucid enough to know what *that* meant. And leaving with Harris wasn't at all what she had in mind. "Um, you know what? I'm not quite ready to go yet," she said quickly.

"Okay, how about another shooter, then?"

"Sure, why not?" Anything to distract him until she could get Adam to come over and give her a ride back home.

Once again, the waitress came by, cap gun in hand, and poured a round of shots for the table. Miranda drank hers down in a single gulp and smiled as she held the empty glass up for all to see. Bobby, Jay, and Kathleen all cheered for her. But Adam didn't. In fact, he seemed to look away the minute she glanced in his direction.

Well, she'd see about that. He *was* going to look at her, damn it. And he was going to do it now! Without a single moment's thought, Miranda leaped up onto the bar. Instantly, all heads turned in her direction.

"Woohoo! You're a wild one!" Harris cheered from his barstool perch at her feet.

"You bet I am," Miranda answered. She began walking across the bar, Coyote Ugly style, moving to the beat of the clapping crowd who'd gathered to cheer her on. She clapped back at them, glancing to see if she'd finally caught Adam's eye.

She'd caught it okay. But as she looked at him, it wasn't love she saw. Not even lust. It was something that looked a lot like disapproval—or disappointment. She was suddenly hit with a sonic boom of overwhelming sadness. She could feel the tears starting. *Oh, no! A crying jag.*

Harris didn't seem to notice. He was all worked up by Miranda's bar walk. "Oh, baby!" he shouted as he reached up and grabbed her leg, trying to pull him toward her. "Come to Papa."

"Whoa!" Miranda tripped over his hand and fell off the bar, landing right on Harris's lap.

That immediately gave him the wrong impression. He leaned down and planted a hot, wet kiss right on Miranda's lips. She struggled to move from his lap, but he held her tight, not allowing her to wrestle herself from his grip or his lips. She began to struggle, moving from side to side, trying to push him away. But she was too drunk. Her arms didn't have the power or control they usually did.

And then, out of nowhere, a strong, familiar arm yanked her free. She looked up into the eyes of her protector. "Adam," she whispered breathlessly. "I knew you'd be there."

"Hey dude, get your own girl," Harris shouted at Adam. "This one's mine."

"Miranda's not anybody's girl," Adam told him.

Miranda blinked back a few tears. *Not anybody's girl.* Here came that crying jag again,

"Get lost," Harris replied. "The lady's with me."

"She's with me now," Adam answered angrily. "And she's going home." He quickly helped her to her feet. She leaned gratefully against his strong shoulder as he led her out of the bar. *Mmm. He felt so safe.*

The night air hit her hard as they left Sally's. The temperature had dipped considerably, and she'd left her jacket inside. "Whoo, sure is chilly tonight," she announced, slurring slightly.

Adam slipped his arms out of his jacket and wrapped it over her shoulders. "Mmm . . . that's better," she cooed. "It smells just like you."

"Come on, I'll call us a cab," he told her.

"Aren't you going to give me a ride on your motorcycle?" She sounded very disappointed.

"Not the way you are tonight," he replied. "You'd fall right off."

"No, you'd take care of me. You *always* take care of me."

"Right. So let's do this my way. We'll take a cab." He pulled out his cell phone and called a cab company.

"Mmmm . . . what a night," Miranda said, raising her face up to the wind. "Whoa. Better not close my eyes. Makes everything spin around."

"What were you thinking having all those shooters?" Adam asked, hanging up the phone and leading her to a nearby bench where they could sit and wait for the taxi's arrival.

"I was just having fun. You know me. Party girl."

"You? A party girl? Since when?" Adam paused and looked at her accusingly. "Since Denny visited?"

Miranda looked at him, surprised.

"Denny? What does he have to do with anything?" She scrunched up her mouth for a minute, thinking. "Oh, my God! You're jealous," she laughed, poking Adam in the shoulder.

"I'm not jealous of anyone."

"Yes, you are. But I don't love Denny. I love somebody else. Do you want to know who?" She was talking a mile a minute, slurring her words together.

"Come on, Miranda, you're drunk."

"Yep. But I can still tell you who I love."

"Okay, so tell me."

"No." Miranda pouted like a little child. "You have to guess."

"I don't want to play games," Adam replied.

"Then you won't find out," Miranda told him. "'Cause you gotta play to win . . . ha-ha-ha." She began giggling hysterically.

"Oh look, here's the cab," Adam said as a taxi pulled up in front of them. He opened the door and literally pushed her inside. He followed her into the car, gave the driver her address, and shut the door.

"You're nice to take me home,"

Miranda murmured, curling up against him. "And I'm glad, 'cuz you haven't been that nice to me lately."

"I haven't?"

"Nope. You hardly talked to me all week. And you disappear all the time. Bobby says you have a girlfriend."

"Bobby says a lot of things."

"Do you?" Miranda demanded.

"Do I what?"

"Have a girlfriend?" She leaned her head back for a minute and grabbed her stomach. "Ooooh," she moaned.

"What's the matter?"

"I don't feel so good. I think I'm gonna throw up."

"Oh, man. Driver, you'd better pull over," Adam shouted to the front seat.

The taxi driver did as he was told. As the car stopped by the curb, Adam opened the door nearest Miranda. She leaned over the side, throwing her guts up into the street. Adam stayed with her, rubbing her back.

"Okay, that's it," she said finally, sitting up.

"You sure?"

Miranda winced. "Yeah. Man my head hurts."

"Wait until tomorrow," Adam predicted. "You're going to have one helluva hangover."

They sat there in silence in the backseat of the cab until they reached Miranda's house. When the car stopped again, Adam paid the driver and hopped out. He helped Miranda to the front door. "Do you have your keys?" he asked her.

She nodded, and reached into the tiny pockets of her shorts. Adam took the key from her and opened the lock. Together, they stepped into the house.

"Oh, I don't feel so good again," Miranda moaned, hightailing it away from Adam and making a mad dash for the bathroom.

Before Adam could follow her, his cell phone rang. He pulled it from his pocket and flipped it open. "Hello?"

"Yo Adam, bro!" Bobby shouted into the receiver. "Where are ya? We're celebratin' down here!"

"I had to bring Miranda home," Adam told him. "She was pretty drunk."

"Yeah. She was totally wasted," Bobby agreed. "I didn't even think she really drank."

"She doesn't," Adam agreed. "Which is why I think the shooters got to her."

"So what made our little Randy get so randy tonight?" Bobby wondered.

"I'm not sure. She said something about being in love."

"With who?"

"I don't know," Adam told him. "But whoever he is, he sure isn't good for her."

Sixteen

The bright Texas sun shone through Miranda's window. She blinked for a minute, trying to adjust her eyes, but it was impossible. Even a second's worth of a glimpse of the light was too painful.

She squinted toward the alarm clock on her nightstand. One o'clock. A surge of panic whipped through her. It wasn't morning after all. It was afternoon. Which meant she'd slept through the review for her English final. Not that she would have been able to focus on what her teacher would be saying, anyway. Not with this headache. Miranda sat up slowly and grabbed the pair of sunglasses that sat beside her clock. She had to brush her teeth. The taste in her mouth was awful.

That's when it all came back to her—the shooters, that jerk Harris, dancing on the bar, and the cab ride home with Adam. Oh, no. The cab ride. She'd thrown up right in front of him. Oh, that must have been quite a sight. Not exactly the kind of seduction she'd been hoping for.

Slowly, she rose to her feet and headed toward the bathroom. Well, there was one bright spot to all this. So much had gone wrong in the past twenty-four hours. It could only be uphill from here.

Or not. As she padded past the stairway, she heard Kathleen and Jay yelling at each other in the living room. The loudness of their voices cut through her head like a sword. But they weren't nearly as painful as the words the two were exchanging.

"I'm not telling Miranda anything," Kathleen screamed. "You can do your own dirty work."

"You're the one who brought her into the band," Jay reminded her.

"And it's a damned good thing I did.

You guys were going nowhere until Miranda joined."

"Joined *temporarily*. Just until Charlie got well. She knew that."

"Yeah, but she's been so good for the band," Kathleen insisted. "You were lucky to have her."

"Hey, we had our material long before Miranda joined. Maybe *she's* the lucky one. She stepped in just when we were on the verge."

"She did not," Kathleen argued. "She made you guys what you are today. And now you want to dump her, just in time for the Austin Jam?"

"Can I help it if Charlie's coming back after Christmas?" Jay countered. "Look, Miranda always knew this day would come."

"If you're so sure of that, why don't you tell her?" Kathleen demanded.

"Because she'll probably cry or something, and I don't want to get into all that female stuff," Jay insisted. "You need to be the one to tell her."

Miranda had heard enough. She hurried down the stairs, her head throbbing with every step. "Neither one of you has to tell me. I heard you. The whole damn world heard you."

Kathleen and Jay stared at her, surprised.

"I'm sorry, Miranda. I thought you were in class," Kathleen apologized.

"Don't feel sorry for me," Miranda assured her. "It's no big deal. And don't worry about my crying, Jay. I'm not gonna cry. I'm not even gonna scream. I'm just going to beat you at your own game."

A few minutes later, Kathleen walked into Miranda's room and sat down in the small chair the girls had found thrown out by the curb. "Are you okay?" she asked quietly.

"You mean the hangover, or being unceremoniously tossed to the side like that chair you're sitting in?"

"The latter," Kathleen replied.

"Well, like Jay said, we always knew it was temporary. I guess I just forgot for a while."

"I was hoping *they'd* forgot," Kathleen said. "You know, it's not completely over. This shouldn't just be up to Jay and Bobby.

I'll bet if we talk to Adam . . . you know how much he likes playing with you."

Adam. Oh, no. There was no way she ever wanted to see him again. "It's all right. I wasn't going to be able to face them again, anyhow," Miranda admitted. "Not after last night."

"Why, because you overdid it on the shooters? That's ridiculous. We've all done that before."

Miranda shook her head and winced. It hurt just to move. "No. It's because I made a complete ass out of myself last night when Adam took me home."

"Adam? Oh, big deal. He's not the kind of guy to judge a girl for drinking too much."

"That's not it," Miranda insisted. "I made a total fool of myself in the car. I almost told him . . ." She stopped herself, not wanting to make a jerk out of herself again.

"Told him what . . . ," she began. Then she glanced at the short-shorts and skimpy top Miranda had slept in, having fallen into bed without getting into pajamas. "Oh. That explains it."

Miranda blushed. "Explains what?"

"The clothes, the highlights in your hair . . . you were trying to get Adam to go to bed with you."

"No. That's not it at all," Miranda insisted. "Not go to bed with me. Just to . . . to . . . notice me."

"Oh, he noticed you last night, all right," Kathleen said. She smiled kindly. "But I wouldn't worry about it. He's not the kind of guy to judge."

"He's not the kind of guy who likes me, either. He made that plenty clear last night. I practically threw myself at him, and he left. He didn't even so much as kiss me."

"He probably didn't want to take advantage of a drunk girl," Kathleen said, and sighed.

"Oh, like he hasn't done that before?" Miranda insisted. "You've seen him with those floozies who show up at Sally's."

"I've seen him flirt a little, sure," Kathleen told her. "But I can't imagine him . . ."

"Yeah. Well, I can. And the thought of it makes me sad, and sick. I'm glad

Charlie's back. I don't want to play with Adam or any guys ever again."

Kathleen sighed. "Please don't give up the drums just because of what happened last night."

"Oh, don't worry about that," Miranda assured her. "I'm not giving up anything. In fact, I'm starting a new band. An *all-girl* band. I know there are two more open slots in that Austin Jam. I'm going to put a band together and get one of those places. And then I'm going to blow the roof off the place. That'll show 'em. I don't need Adam. I don't need Sin-Phony. I got everything right here." She pointed proudly to her drumsticks.

"Not exactly," Kathleen reminded her.

"What? Are you taking *their* side now?"

"No way. I'm plenty pissed at Jay. It's just that you don't have everything you need . . . not yet, anyway."

"Why, what don't I have?"

"How about a singer, a guitarist, and a bass player, for starters?"

Miranda nodded. "True. But somehow I think that somewhere in this big city there are some 'chick' musicians who really want to play. All I have to do is find them."

After Kathleen left her room, Miranda forced herself to take a good look in her mirror. Long black streaks of mascara had run down her cheeks, like prison bars over her skin. Her hair was all over the place, and the shorts and shirt were a wrinkled mess. It was not a pretty sight.

Miranda sighed. This just wasn't her. Maybe Missy was happy parading around in too much makeup and too little clothes, but that just wasn't Miranda. Besides, if looking like Missy attracted guys like those losers at the bar last night, she'd be better off without any man at all.

There was just one thing to do! Miranda threw open her dresser drawers and began dumping all of the new clothes on the floor. She'd be donating those to Mother's wardrobe. The plaster-of-Paris momma needed a new look more than Miranda did. Miranda was fine just the way she was.

Well, *almost*. She was definitely keeping the highlights in her hair. She loved those. They were kind of fun. And a girl needs that now and again.

Especially now.

On the following Monday, a freshly high-lighted, and extremely exhausted, Miranda sat behind the drums in the small studio and rested her head in her hands. "How many bad guitarists does that make?" she moaned.

"I lost count at the girl who had to check her fingering after each chord," Kathleen replied.

"This is ridiculous. Whatever gave me the idea that I could put a band together anyway?"

Kathleen shrugged. "Guts? Anger? Revenge?"

"More like all of the above," Miranda told her. She looked down at the sheet of paper at her feet. "Who's next?"

"Keyboardist at three o'clock," Kathleen told her.

"I hope she's good. I'm sick of smiling on the outside and grimacing on the inside."

A few minutes later, a tall, muscular girl in running pants and sneakers knocked on the door. She carried a big suitcase by her side.

"You must be the keyboardist," Miranda greeted her. She stood up from behind her drums and held out her hand. "I'm Miranda."

"I'm Chrissy," the girl told her.

Miranda had to choke back a laugh. Despite her tall, muscular build, Chrissy had a tiny squeaky voice, sort of like Minnie Mouse. "Well, I don't know how much Kathleen told you on the phone about the band I want to put together, but I'm looking for a kind of unique sound," Miranda explained.

"I know exactly what you mean," Chrissy assured her. "I'm not into the run-of-the-mill stuff you hear in clubs. I go for something more interesting." She plopped her large suitcase on the counter.

"Um . . . what do you have in there?" Miranda asked curiously. She'd certainly never seen a keyboard come out of one of those before.

"It's my accordion," Chrissy announced. She swung the hand-held keyboard over her shoulders and began squeezing the box in and out. "I've written a whole lot of tunes for it. Check this one out. It's an original." Suddenly, the sounds of a polka began to emit from the accordion. Then, before Kathleen or Miranda could stop her, Chrissy began to dance around the room, doing some strange interpretive folk dance to the music. "Come on, don't you want to jam to this?" she asked Miranda.

Not wanting to hurt Chrissy's feelings, Miranda tried her best to capture the beat of Chrissy's tune. But the rhythm seemed to be changing throughout the song, and Miranda had absolutely no experience with polka music. Thankfully, after a while, Chrissy stopped and frowned. "You know," she told Miranda honestly, "I don't think this is gonna work for me. You're just not enough of a drummer for my stuff."

"Excuse *you?*" Kathleen bellowed, rising to every inch of her six menacing feet. "I'll have you know that Miranda is a kick-ass drummer! Nobody rocks like she does."

"That's fine, if all you want to do is rock," Chrissy explained. "My music is much more innovative."

"That's one way to describe it," Kathleen replied dismissively.

"You know, I think Chrissy is right,"

Miranda told Kathleen. "Our styles don't mesh."

"Exactly," Chrissy agreed. "I couldn't have said it better." She packed her accordion back into its case. "Well, I gotta go. "

She wasn't two feet out the door when Miranda and Kathleen exploded into a fit of laughter. "Do you believe her?" Kathleen gasped between giggles. "I mean what was this?" She began stomping her big black boots across the floor in an imitation of Chrissy's interpretive polka.

"Well, at least we got a laugh out of all this," Miranda said, giggling as Kathleen continued her dance.

"We'll get more than that. You haven't met Althea yet."

"Althea?"

"Yeah. She's a girl I met in a mosh pit at a concert last summer. She has the most amazing voice. She's coming at three fifteen. Prepare to be blown away."

Sure enough, at 3:15 on the dot, a petite girl with long brown braids, pale white skin, and just a touch of pink lipstick appeared at the door. Kathleen raced over and hugged her. "Althea!" she greeted her friend.

"Hi, Kat. I hope I'm not late."

Miranda stared at the two girls. They couldn't have been more different if they'd tried. Tall, dark Kathleen, all in black, and tiny, clean-scrubbed Althea, all dressed in pale pink and jeans. It was hard to believe the two were friends, never mind the fact that Kathleen had met someone like Althea in a mosh pit. "Hi. I'm Miranda," she introduced herself finally.

"I'm Althea. Kathleen has told me so much about you. I hope we can work together."

"We don't have the other girls squared away yet," Kathleen warned her friend. "So far, it's just you and Miranda."

"That's cool," Althea said. "Is there anything special y'all want me to sing?

"No," Miranda told her. "Whatever makes you most comfortable."

Althea took her guitar from its case and strapped it over her shoulder. Then she sipped some water from the bottle she'd carried in with her and began to sing. "Busted flat in Baton Rouge, waiting on a train. I was feeling near as faded as my jeans . . ."

Miranda and Kathleen both sat there mesmerized, as Althea put her own unique spin on the old Janis Joplin hit, "Me and Bobby McGee." Janis Joplin was a legend in Austin, being a Texas girl herself, and almost everyone in the state had been raised on her soulful, bluesy sound. At that moment, Miranda truly believed that Althea would someday hold that status as well. But, judging from her clean-cut appearance, she would do it without all the boozing and drugging that eventually had killed Janis.

"Oh, my goodness, that was unbelievable," Miranda told her as the song came to an end.

"I'd say we've found our lead singer," Kathleen announced.

"*And* our guitarist," Miranda added. She picked up her sticks. "You want to try and play a little more Janis with me?"

"Okay," Althea agreed. "How about 'Try'? Do you know that one?"

"Sure," Miranda replied. "Let's go."

The two musicians began to jam, with Miranda on drums and background vocals and Althea on guitar and lead. They sounded wonderful, although something was definitely missing.

"It's the bass," Miranda finally said, ruefully recalling the powerful rhythm section she and Adam had once formed. "We need a bass player." She turned to Kathleen. "Didn't Missy say she was sending over a friend from her applied mathematical theories class who plays the bass?"

"Oh great. Just what we need. A math-geek bass player," Kathleen snarled. "This should be good."

"Who says she's a geek? Missy's a math whiz, remember? And *she's* no geek."

"Missy is an aberration," Kathleen insisted.

"We have to give her a chance," Miranda told her. "Maybe she'll really rock."

"Miranda's right," Althea agreed. "You never know."

"Oh, yeah, a rockin' math major," Kathleen laughed. "Like that'll happen."

Despite Kathleen's doubts, Miranda was determined to keep an open mind about Missy's friend. She had to. She'd spent her entire week's money on renting out the studio space for these auditions. She couldn't afford to do it again. They had to get the band together today.

But as Missy's friend walked into the room, Miranda's hopes were dashed. The bassist—a tall, African-American girl with short hair and glasses—wasn't carrying a guitar case strapped over her back. Rather, she wheeled in a large plastic case that stood nearly as tall as she did. *Oh please, not another weirdo like that accordionist.*

"What's that?" Kathleen asked her pointedly. She was obviously thinking the same thing.

"My bass," the girl replied. She held out a firm hand to Kathleen. "I'm Chelsea. You must be Miranda."

"No, I'm Kathleen, the band manager."

Miranda looked at her with surprise. She had no idea Kathleen considered herself the manager. *Oh, boy.* Jay wasn't going to like that one bit.

"That's Miranda," Kathleen continued, "the drummer and founder of the group. And this is Althea, our lead singer and guitarist."

Chelsea turned and smiled at Miranda

and Althea. "I'm Chelsea. Missy mentioned in class the other day that you were putting together a group and that you needed a bassist, so I thought I'd come by and chat." She opened the case and pulled out a stand-up bass—the kind they play in orchestras.

Before Miranda could get a word in, Kathleen shook her head. "I don't know how much Missy told you, but this isn't some chamber orchestra. We're lookin' to rock the place."

"Oh," Chelsea said quietly, obviously a bit overwhelmed by Kathleen's harshness. "Well . . . I . . ." She began to put the bass back in the case.

"Wait, don't do that," Miranda urged. "You know, I have this idea. My mom used to listen to this eighties rockabilly band, The Stray Cats. And they had a stand-up bass player in the band." She turned to Chelsea. "It's a little different from the way you play classical bass, but if you can pluck to the beat, maybe we could have a really unique sound."

"Yeah! My folks used to listen to them too." Althea agreed. "But I haven't seen a stand-up bass in any group here in Austin."

"Cool!" Miranda exclaimed. "It could be something no one else has."

"I can give it a try," Chelsea agreed.

"Uh, guys . . . ," Kathleen began with skepticism. But Miranda and Althea were already into the new idea.

"Do you know 'Stray Cat Strut'?" Althea asked Miranda.

"Sure," Miranda agreed. She turned to Chelsea. "Just join in when you're ready."

It took a few minutes for Chelsea to catch on to the sound, but it was obvious that she was a trained musician, when she quickly picked up the beat and the chords. And while she seemed unsure of herself, it soon became clear to everyone—even Kathleen—that this was the sound they'd been looking for.

Rehearsals were a top priority for the group—especially if they wanted to be in any shape by the time the Austin Jam rolled around. And that was easier said than done, because although all the girls were talented, they were having a bit of trouble getting their musical styles to gel. Miranda had wanted to have a band of equals—no leader. She'd never liked the way Jay had taken over that role because he was the singer in Sin-Phony. But without a leader, the girls often found themselves running off in different directions—with Althea sometimes adding some odd harmonies to her vocals, or Chelsea and Miranda going off on a rhythmic riff of their own. It was at those times especially that she missed Adam. They may not have been meant for each other romantically, but musically, they'd always been in tune.

Which was what she struggled to explain to Cally one afternoon after rehearsal. She'd managed to catch her best friend between her film classes and her usual midday surf. Cally was caught up in the California life—and getting a chance to talk with her was becoming more and more difficult.

"I miss Adam all the time, but especially when I'm drumming," Miranda told her. "It's like there's a hole or something, and I can't fill it."

"Wow! I hadn't realized you and Adam had actually hooked up," Cally replied. "I guess I should have called you more often."

"We didn't hook up or anything," Miranda explained, not arguing with Cally's admission of guilt about not returning phone calls. "He never saw me that way. But . . ." She stopped herself, considering what Cally had said. "I guess you're right. It's like I'm mourning the end of a romance that never happened. And you can't mourn something you never had, can you?"

"Who says you never had it?" Cally asked.

"I just told you: Adam wasn't into me like that," Miranda repeated.

"Not in this life, maybe. But it's possible you two were lovers in a past life, and you're trying to find each other again."

"What are you talking about?" Miranda asked.

"Reincarnation," Cally told her. "My psychic is really into it. She said I was probably an explorer back in the fourteen hundreds. It's in my spirit to cross new frontiers."

Miranda was glad Cally couldn't see the way she was rolling her eyes right now. Psychics? Reincarnation? "Come on, Cal," she said. "You're kidding, right?"

"You've got to open your mind, Miranda," Cally admonished her. "You can't enjoy this life until you make peace with the lives you experienced before. Now, I'm going to give my psychic all your information—your birthday and stuff. Maybe she can give you some insight into Adam. Of course, I'll need his birthdate too. Do you know it?"

Obviously Cally wasn't going to be much help. "I don't know. Which birthdate do you mean?" Miranda asked wryly. "In this life, or in his last one?"

Miranda had no choice but to put Adam out of her mind. He was just muddying the waters. Frankly, she had to do well on her finals to keep up her partial scholarship. And she needed to focus on the band, as well. There was simply no point in harping on the impossible.

The strategy seemed to work. Her finals seemed okay—if a little tougher than she'd anticipated. And with each rehearsal, the band got better and better. The girls were learning to work together, playing off one another's strengths, and compensating for weaknesses. The music was working. But so far, no one had heard them, besides themselves. It seemed highly unlikely that, without any live performances, they'd ever get a spot in the Austin Jam.

Luckily, as band manager, Kathleen felt *that* was her responsibility. And, after all her time hanging out with Jay and the other guys in Sin-Phony, she had plenty of connections. By the time the second week of winter break rolled around, she was able to call Miranda at home in Barton with the good news.

"You got us a gig based on that one little tape?" Miranda was incredulous, especially considering the tape had been made on a tiny little recorder Missy had loaned them.

"The tape, *and* my charm," Kathleen laughed. "I called in a few favors. But don't be so excited. It's the first band slot of the evening. It's kind of early. I don't know how many people will be there."

"I don't care," Miranda shouted excitedly. "*We'll* be there! *At the Austin Jam.* And it's all thanks to you." She stopped herself, realizing what Kathleen may have sacrificed when she'd switched her loyalty to Miranda's new band. "How'd Jay take the news?"

"He just kind of shrugged it off. After all, they have a better time slot." Kathleen sighed. "Besides, it doesn't matter. I don't know how much longer Jay and I have as a couple. He's kind of juvenile. I may be looking for greener pastures soon."

"Oh. I'm sorry."

"Don't be," Kathleen told her. "I never planned on marrying the guy. Besides, there's this amazing graduate assistant who teaches my advertising layout class. I'd like to get to know *his* layout a little better."

Miranda giggled. "You're one of a kind, Kathleen."

"And the world's luckier for it," Kathleen joked. "So how'd you make out with your Christmas gifts?"

"Amazing!" Miranda exclaimed. "My folks gave me a few pairs of new drumsticks, and money for practice rooms. Cally gave me this T-shirt that says 'Drummers Do It to the Beat.'"

"Subtle," Kathleen laughed.

Miranda giggled too. "Yeah, it's not exactly my style."

"Well, I'm glad you know what your style is, now," Kathleen said knowingly.

"Mm-hmm," Miranda agreed. "My mom was a little shocked at the streaks in my hair, but imagine how she would have taken some of those outfits Missy put together."

"Sort of like the first time I came home with my hair dyed black and my big-heeled boots."

Miranda sighed. She could only picture what *that* homecoming must have been like.

"Well, listen, I gotta—" Kathleen began.

"Wait," Miranda urged her. "I almost forgot the best news of all. My mom came up with the most awesome name for the band!"

"What?"

"Okay, here goes," Miranda said, taking a huge breath. "The name of our band is . . . the Purple Garters."

Seventeen

About a week before classes started, Miranda came back to Austin so the Purple Garters would have enough time to rehearse before the Austin Jam. The girls got together and put together a set list that included a few classics by old time Rockabilly heroes like Chet Atkins and Jerry Lee Lewis, and they'd managed to write two original instrumental tunes that really rocked the house. By the time the night of the Austin Jam came around, they'd managed to put together a really tight—albeit *short*—set of songs. Not bad for a band that had only been together about a month.

The girls had all agreed to meet at Miranda and Kathleen's house and go over to the club as a band, in the hopes that they wouldn't be so nervous if they were all together. It was a good, logical plan. Unfortunately, it didn't work. The band members—and Kathleen, for that matter—were just as nervous together as they'd been apart. In fact, their collective nervous energy was overwhelming. None of the girls seemed to be able to sit still long enough for Missy to do her hair and makeup. Miranda's skin tone was turning the odd color of green one gets right before she pukes, which was hardly a good match for her highlighted blond hair. Miranda *loved* those highlights, which were the only remnant of her Get-Adam scheme. But right now what she really would have loved was some air. "I need to get out of here," she shouted, suddenly leaping up and heading for the door.

"Hey, watch it," Missy cried out, leaping to catch Mother after Miranda accidentally bumped into her.

"Oh, sorry," Miranda said.

"Don't apologize to me," Missy said. "It's Mother you banged into."

Miranda turned to the mannequin, who was currently dressed in Miranda's man-catching denim short-shorts and a tight shirt. "Sorry, Mother."

"That's better," Missy joked with a smile. "You know what you need?"

"What?"

"A good yoga session." She got down on the floor and began to contort her body in an almost inhuman position.

"No time for that now," Kathleen announced, pulling Miranda toward the door. "We gotta go."

"Wait a minute! You forgot your garters!" Missy cried out. She quickly handed each girl what looked like a purple satin scrunchy.

"Right or left leg?" Althea asked.

"I don't think it matters," Missy told her. "As long as you're all wearing them. They're your trademarks—like those chicken feet the Dixie Chicks got tattooed on their ankles. One for each number-one hit."

Number-one hit? She'd settle for just getting through this night without passing out. Miranda slid the garter over the right leg of her faded Levi's, and took a deep breath. "Okay, this is it," she said as she headed for the door. "The debut of the Purple Garters."

The girls arrived at the club at around 7:30, giving them just enough time to get set up and do a sound check. Miranda was impressed with the drum set. Unlike the old, broken-down equipment at Sally's, the producers of the Austin Jam had come through with a kick-butt drum kit, certainly the best she'd played on. She sat down and gleefully began banging on the snare while hitting the bass pedal with her foot. "Oh, sweet!" she exclaimed.

"Not as sweet as you are," a familiar voice bellowed from the door of the club.

Miranda looked up suddenly. "Oh, my God! Jerry!" she squealed, leaping up from her drums and running over to give the big guy a massive hug.

"Hey there, Rand!" he said, scooping her up in his meaty arms and twirling her around. "It's been too damn long, you know that?"

"I can't believe you're here. How'd you know?"

"I saw the list of performers in the paper. Your name's in there, under the Purple Garters."

"That's my band."

Jerry laughed. "I kind of figured. Anyhow, I'm here to check out what you've been up to since you left the shop."

"A lot," Miranda told him. "I've been playing at Sally's Pub on Wednesdays with Sin-Phony. Or at least I used to. Their original drummer came back, and I was out. But, now . . ."

"Now you're a Garter girl," Jerry teased, reaching down and thwacking the purple garter around her leg.

"Yeah," Miranda said, laughing. "That's me."

Jerry cleared his throat. "I tried to get Paul to come tonight, but . . ."

"But he wasn't interested in hearing a college-girl band, right?"

Jerry smirked. "Something like that."

"It's all right. I've put him way behind me."

"Jackie's meeting me in a bit, though," Jerry told her. "She's that waitress from Jessup's. The one who got me the passes one night. Remember?"

Miranda nodded. That was the night Paul had made her stay behind to lock up the store. The night he'd bumped into Amber. It was a distant memory now, at best.

Jerry smiled proudly. "Jackie and I are an item now."

"Good for you," Miranda told him. "She's a lucky girl."

"No, *I'm* the lucky one," Jerry answered. "So I gotta keep her happy. I'm gonna get us a good table. You'd better get backstage. You're on in a few minutes."

"Okay, I'll see you after the set."

"You'd better," Jerry told her.

Miranda turned and raced backstage to the other girls. "Kathleen! Did you see who came?" she asked her friend.

"Yeah," Kathleen said slowly. "Are you okay with it?"

"Sure. Why wouldn't I be okay with seeing Jerry again?"

"Jerry?" Kathleen sounded confused.

"Who's Jerry? I was talking about Adam. Didn't you see him come in?"

Miranda gasped. "Adam's here?"

"Yeah, he got here, like, two minutes ago."

"Why? Sin-Phony's not on till four a.m."

Kathleen shrugged. "Maybe he came to hear *your* band."

"*Oh, no.* I don't want him to hear us!"

"Why?" Kathleen asked. "You guys rock."

"I know, but . . . I'm so embarrassed. You don't know how I acted when—"

"Oh, I have an idea," Kathleen assured her. "But hey, it's ancient history. He's probably forgotten all about it by now."

But Miranda knew *she* never would forget. As hard as she tried, Adam was never far from her mind. While she was playing, she wondered how he might have enhanced the rhythm of a tune. Whenever she saw a motorcycle pass by, she thought about their rides through the streets of Austin. And when she closed her eyes at night, his was the last face she thought of. Which could explain why he was all over her dreams.

Adam wasn't ancient history to her. Not by a long shot. For the rest of her life she'd judge every guy she met by how he measured up to Adam.

"I can't do this," she whispered to Kathleen. "I can't play with him here. You gotta get rid of him."

"No way, babe. That's not happenin'. You're a professional. Now get out there and hit the skins. You're gonna rock this house!"

A *professional*? Kathleen was exaggerating more than slightly—as she was apt to do. Still, it was kind of cool hearing someone call her that. The word was enough to get Miranda onto the stage.

"Ladies and gentlemen! Our first band of the night. Let's give a huge Austin Jam welcome to the Purple Garters."

The spotlights burst on, and suddenly all eyes and ears were on Miranda, Chelsea, and Althea. Miranda was grateful for the hot lights—it made it impossible to see the audience. It wasn't a huge crowd—most people were coming later so they could be awake and partying when the more known bands arrived—but there were quite a few folks out there. Miranda could tell by the way they stomped their feet as the girls let loose with their own kick-ass version of Carl Perkins's "Honey Don't." It seemed the audience was really taken with the girls' sound: a true Texas combination of R & B and bluegrass. It was magical being onstage again. And it was even better this time, because she'd been with this group from the start. This was *her* band. *Her* music.

The foot-stomping cheers of the audience raced through her veins like a drug, giving her the most incredible high. It was the ultimate power trip. She was making these people scream and dance, and sing along. They loved her, and she loved them back. She knew for sure that she was addicted to the music, the club scene, and the applause. This was what she was meant to do.

Her heart pounded wildly as the Purple Garters ended their set. She raced off the stage, getting a quick hug from Kathleen before racing toward the tables. People were swarming her, complimenting her on her drumming, and the band itself.

Miranda was warm, smiling, and thankful for their praise. But she really just wanted them to get out of her way.

The ego boost the performance gave her was enough to provide Miranda with the strength she needed to talk to Adam. She was ready to face him, talk to him, and calmly—*soberly*—let the chips fall where they may. She had to have closure on this thing, one way or another. Things seemed to be going her way tonight. Maybe she was on a lucky streak. Maybe Adam had been missing her, too. He had to have been. Why else would he have come to hear her play?

"Miranda, that was awesome!" Jerry greeted her as she passed his table. He stood up and gave her a huge hug. Any other time that would have been great—a hug from an old friend was always welcome. But today, Jerry's big body was like a giant, unmovable mountain coming between Adam and herself.

"Thanks," she said, trying to sound appreciative.

"I didn't know you could sing like

that," Jerry told her, releasing her from his grip.

"Well, we all sing a little. Mostly that's Althea's job, though. I just do backup harmonies," Miranda told him humbly, her eyes darting around the club as she spoke.

"Can we buy you a drink?" Jerry asked. "It's fifteen minutes till the next act, so we can sit a spell and catch up. I want to hear all about the Purple Garters."

Miranda looked over and smiled at the small, petite girl who was Jerry's date. "Oh, now Jackie doesn't want to listen to all that."

"I don't mind," Jackie assured her. "I thought you guys were awesome. I'd love to get an all-girl band together someday. But I'm not much of a team player. I'm more the solo type."

Jerry reached down and squeezed her petite shoulder. "Or the duo type—right, hon?"

Jackie laughed. "You know what I mean."

Miranda smiled at the two of them. They seemed so happy. Her eyes looked around the room again, searching for

Adam, hoping that they, too, had a chance for something like that. But she didn't see him anywhere.

A deep shroud of sadness and regret came over her, wiping away the joy she'd felt just minutes before. Adam was gone. Somehow, without him to share it with, her triumphant return to the stage didn't seem that huge of a deal anymore.

Eighteen

"Look, you guys, I'm beat," Miranda told her roommates as she stood and moved away from the table in the back of the bar where she, Kathleen, and Missy had planted themselves for the rest of the Austin Jam. It was three thirty in the morning, and she was definitely fading. The rush of the Purple Garters' eight o'clock gig was long since gone. In fact, Althea and Chelsea had left hours ago.

"Come on, Rand, you gotta stay and hear Sin-Phony," Kathleen urged her. "Adam came to hear *you.*"

"Yeah well, he obviously didn't like what he heard."

"You don't know that," Kathleen countered. "There's a million reasons he could've left."

"Nah. He hated it. He isn't too fond of me, either."

"If that's true, he's the only one," Missy assured her. "This crowd was going wild for you. Your drum solo was totally insane. Bill was blown away."

"Then why'd he leave?" Miranda asked pointedly.

"He went home because he had a squash match tomorrow."

Kathleen chuckled. "It's weird to think of you dating a guy from the squash team."

"You think *that's* weird? How about the fact that I'm finally with a guy whose hair I can run my fingers through," Missy replied with a giggle. "No more nubby scalps for me."

"Come on, let's have one more round," Kathleen said. "I'll buy the pitcher. You can at least hang out long enough to hear one or two songs."

Miranda sighed. "Well, if you're buying . . ."

"That's the spirit!" Kathleen said. "Just

remember, as your manager, I'll be making ten percent of whatever the Purple Garters earn. So basically, I'm spending your money, right?"

"If we start earning money, I'll gladly turn it over," Miranda assured her.

"Good, because there's this car I've been eyeing . . ."

"Ooh! A car!" Missy got excited. "We could all drive to campus together. What kind of car is it?"

"A used hearse," Kathleen replied. "I saw an ad for it in the paper. Doesn't that sound cool?"

A shiver went up and down Miranda's spine. "Cool" wasn't exactly the word that came to mind.

"Okay, ladies and gentlemen," the emcee shouted into his mike. "Here they are, straight from Sally's Pub. Give it up for Sin-Phony."

The band opened their show with "Massacre of the Heart." Miranda listened as Jay sang the words Adam had written. He sounded angrier than usual, as though he were a captured animal crying out in pain. It added a new sort of sincerity to his sound. Miranda figured that probably had something to do with the recent breakup of his relationship with Kathleen. If nothing else, the pain in his love life had improved his music immensely.

She was far less impressed with Charlie's drumming, though. Not that she was bitter or anything. Charlie just wasn't that great of a drummer. He was able to keep the beat, but that was it. There were no nuances, no innovative jams with Adam. She couldn't help but feel just slightly superior.

"Okay, this next tune is a new one," Jay announced to the audience as "Massacre" came to a close. "It's called 'Texas Rose.'"

The song opened slowly, with a keyboard introduction. Jay added a sad guitar riff, and Charlie hit his drums softly. And then, the strangest thing happened: Instead of Jay singing, Adam stepped up to the mike.

"She was my yellow Texas rose," he sang. "A soft petaled beauty, who never thought to pose. She let me be myself, I could trust her with my soul. I knew she'd treat it gently, for only she could make me whole. Her honesty and strength made her rise above the garden. Her genuine Texas sweetness, I never thought would harden . . ."

Suddenly, the mood shifted. Charlie banged on his drums, Adam plucked violently at the strings of his bass, Bobby hit some harsh keyboard chords, and Jay let out a face-melting stream of notes from his guitar.

"And then it changed," Adam shouted into mike. "My Texas rose grew thorns. Beneath her leather cowboy hat, my darlin' angel had horns. She went from cowboy boots to heels. Started spinning other guys' wheels . . ."

Miranda gasped, suddenly understanding why it had been so important to Kathleen that she stay and hear Sin-Phony. Her roommate had been aware of the new band's set list, and she'd wanted to make sure Miranda heard this song.

It all began to make sense. Now she knew why Adam had so suddenly disappeared from her life; why he hadn't made any attempt to keep her in the band, even though it was obvious she was the better drummer. The new Miranda, the one she and Missy had created, was painful for him to watch in action.

Miranda stared pointedly at Missy. Her roommate—the big expert on men—had been completely wrong about Adam. He wasn't looking for some sex kitten, after all. He'd wanted to give his heart to a genuine Texas rose—a girl like Miranda *really* was. If she hadn't listened to Missy, if she hadn't tried to change . . . *no.* She couldn't blame Missy. There was only one person to blame for what had happened between her and Adam, and that was Miranda Lockheart.

As she sat there, listening to Adam sing, only one thought ran through Miranda's mind. She was desperate to show him that her days of tight jeans, stiletto heels, and dancing on bars were over. The real Miranda, the small-town girl who would rather shoot hoops than hit the sales racks at the mall, and who preferred drinking iced tea to shooters any day, was here to stay. It wasn't worth changing to please someone else. She wanted to be loved for herself. And, *at least for a while,* Adam had fallen for the person she really was.

If only he would believe that the bloom wasn't completely off this Texas rose.

Sin-Phony ended its set with "Same Old, Same Old." Miranda sighed at the irony— if she'd only remained the *same old* girl. . . . Then she shook her head. That wasn't true either. Nothing really stayed the same. Not completely. Sure, she was still Miranda Lockheart from Barton, Texas, the same old girl who'd come to Austin just a few months before. But she'd changed too. She was more open to people who were different, and she'd learned to survive on her own. Hell, she'd even learned to have lunch all by herself in the student center without caring whether people were staring at her and wondering whether she had any friends. She didn't particularly care what other people thought. And that was a big change from the high school Miranda who'd arrived in Austin just six months before.

Most importantly, she taken up the drums and found a true passion. So while some things had remained the same, others were changed forever.

She'd just gone a little overboard in the change department for a while there.

But that was all over now, and she was anxious to let Adam know that. So, as soon as the lights went down on the stage, Miranda hurried over to congratulate the boys.

"Hey, Rand," Bobby greeted her. "What'd you think?"

"You were really good," Miranda replied. There, that was the truth. Bobby had sounded good, as had Jay and Adam. But, Charlie . . .

"Hey, Charlie—come here," Bobby said, calling over to the drummer.

"No, that's okay . . . ," Miranda began.

"You two gotta meet," Bobby continued as Charlie, a gaunt, pale guy with black and yellow stripes in his long hair, sauntered over toward the edge of the stage. "This is Miranda," Bobby introduced her. "The girl who took your seat for a little bit while you were out."

"Hey," Charlie mumbled, shoving his hands into his pockets.

"Hey," Miranda replied, equally uncomfortable. She looked up and saw Jay and Adam standing near each other, putting their guitars away. "I'm gonna go congratulate the other guys, 'kay?" she told Bobby.

"Sure. See ya later."

Miranda nodded, and then took a deep breath before walking around to the other side of the stage. "Howdy," she said, trying to sound cool, calm, and collected as she greeted the guys.

"Hey, Rand," Jay replied. "Congrats on getting on the program. I heard you guys kicked butt."

Miranda smiled. He had to have heard that from Adam. He was giving her compliments. Okay, that was a good sign. "Thanks. You guys were great, too." She forced a shaky smile to her lips. "Hi, Adam," she said softly.

Adam looked down at her, his brown eyes searching her face for something, she wasn't sure what. "Hi, Miranda," he said quietly.

"Um, I'm glad you finally sang one of your own songs."

"Hey!" Jay interrupted.

"Oh, I didn't mean anything by that,"

Miranda assured him, embarrassed. "You sounded great tonight. It's just that Adam puts a different spin on things, and sometimes . . ."

"There are some songs I don't want anyone else singing," Adam explained. "Some of them are too much a part of me."

Miranda nodded. "Well, it was an amazing song. The lyrics really got to me."

"Did they?" Adam asked, a small glimmer of hope in his tone.

"Yeah," she said softly. "You say things beautifully. Words come to you so easily."

"That one wasn't so easy to write . . . or to live through," Adam replied.

Jay looked from Adam to Miranda and back again. Their eyes were locked, so focused on each other that they didn't seem to notice anyone else in the room. "Well, I'm outta here," he said, taking his guitar and hightailing it off the stage.

"I, um, I liked your set," Adam said, finally filling the dead air between them.

"Yeah. The band's a good fit for me."

"I'm glad you found your music," Adam told her.

Miranda frowned. Was this all they

were going to talk about? Music? There was so much more they needed to talk about. So much left unsaid. She couldn't let it stay that way. Not again. "You . . . you want to take a walk?" she asked in a voice so low, he could barely hear her.

"Sure," he answered in just as quiet a tone.

They stood outside the club for a moment, the cold night air shaking them from their trance. Miranda pulled her brown suede jacket tightly around her. "I wanted to thank you for bringing me home that night." She winced slightly. That wasn't at all what she'd wanted to say. But the other stuff was so hard to put into words.

"It's okay," he replied.

"No. It's not," Miranda told him sincerely. "I made a total ass out of myself and you came along and saved me from . . . from . . ."

"It's really no big deal, Miranda."

"Yes, it is. It's a huge deal. Because after that night, you stopped talking to me. So something I did must've really pissed you off."

"No. That's not it," he said slowly.

"Then why'd you just blow me off?"

"Look, Miranda," he started, searching for just the right words. "The thing is, I thought you and I had a good thing going. I thought we'd made a connection. And then Denny came . . ."

"Denny? What does he have to do with anything?"

"I don't know. You tell me. After he visited, everything changed."

"Denny *did* change everything," Miranda admitted.

Adam's face fell. "I figured. You and Denny . . ."

Miranda shook her head wildly. "There is no me and Denny. His visit changed things because I realized how I felt about *you*. Seeing Denny made me realize that I didn't feel anything for him. Not really. It had been puppy love, if that. But *you*—the way I *felt* about you—that was the real thing. Unfortunately, you didn't even know I was alive. So I thought, if I wore different clothes . . ." Miranda took a deep breath, as if trying to catch the words before they left her mouth. But she couldn't take them back. She'd said it now. There was nothing she could do but wait and see how Adam reacted.

"Didn't know you were alive?" Adam sounded incredulous. "Are you nuts? Couldn't you see that *I* only seemed to come alive when you were around? I've been crazy about you since we met, Miranda. But you didn't give me any sign that you wanted anything more than a friend. And so I told myself I was happy with that. Then, when you started dressing and acting so weird, I figured that was the way Denny likes his women and that you and he were working things out."

"I told everyone it was over between us."

"People say a lot of things. But their actions sometimes show something else. I got all confused. I'd seen people change like that before, and . . ."

Miranda frowned. He was talking about *Joni*. She'd gone to New York City and come back a fashion-forward sophisticate on the cocktail party circuit. He'd been afraid that Miranda was changing just the way Joni had—well, not in the exact same way, but in a way that made him feel like she was moving away from him. "We should have been more honest with each other. We would have saved ourselves a lot of pain." She laughed ruefully. "And I would have saved a whole heck of a lot of cash on that trashy wardrobe."

Adam smiled. "You could still wear a few of those things in private, couldn't you?"

"You never know."

Adam sighed. "It seems like you and I have wasted an awful lot of time."

Miranda nodded, and opened her mouth to speak. But before she could get the words out, Adam pulled her close and kissed her hard. He had no intention of wasting another moment.

She felt the warmth of his lips joining together with her own and the power of his strong arms clutching her body closer and closer until not even air could fit between their chests. He stroked her cheek lightly, as though wanting to make sure that she was really there and was not some dream. She ran her fingers through his long brown hair, finally fulfilling a fantasy she'd been harboring for weeks. As they kissed, she tried to memorize everything about the moment: the taste of his warm, sensitive lips; the cool, gentle touch of his hand against her face; the slightly musky scent of his aftershave. And with each flicker of his tongue against hers, Miranda's heart beat so wildly, she thought it might burst through her chest. She wasn't alone in that. Even through the thickness of his leather jacket, she could feel Adam's heart thumping as passionately as her own.

The beating of their hearts was in perfect sync. Not that Miranda would have expected it to be any other way. She and Adam had always been able to merge their rhythms together into one. And now, although they were in separate bands, they were creating a rhythm section of their own. One that would surely last a lifetime.

About the Author

Nancy Krulik is the author of more than one hundred books for children and young adults. She has written biographies of many of today's major celebrities, including the *New York Times* bestselling *Leonardo DiCaprio: A Biography*. Nancy lives in Manhattan with her husband, composer and drummer Daniel Burwasser, their two children, Ian and Amanda, and a crazed cocker spaniel named Pepper.

LOL at this sneak peek of
30 Guys in 30 Days
By Micol Ostow

A New Romantic Comedy from Simon Pulse

"I can't believe you just went home," Charlie said.

It was the evening after the frat party and we were sitting in the dining hall picking at dinner and rehashing the events of the previous night. Or, rather, I was listlessly picking away. Charlie was wolfing down her sandwich with gusto. She swatted at my hand as I reached for another fry.

"Hey!" I protested.

"I'm hungry. There are plenty more fries over at the steam table."

I shook my head. "Not gonna happen." I sunk lower into my seat and zipped up the front of my hoodie. "Tired."

She nodded. "Well, you had a long night," she agreed. "And with a sad ending."

I stabbed my fork toward my salad, chasing a cherry tomato around the bowl. "It was stupid to think Mr. Co-ed Naked could replace Drew."

"Maybe it's too soon to be looking to replace Drew," Charlie offered carefully. "If you're feeling like your sex appeal is on the fritz, maybe you need to get more practice in. Co-ed Naked might have been a dork-wad, but talking to him did loosen you up. Baby steps."

"So what am I supposed to do, talk to someone new every day?" I grumbled. "File a report with the flirt police?"

"Yes! Well, I mean, not quite," Charlie said, sounding thoughtful. "You don't have to file a report. But you should do that. One guy a day. For thirty days. You know, 'thirty days hath September.' It could be your September thing."

"That's a lot of days," I muttered. "And anyway, it's September third. We're already behind."

"Whatever. It's a good, round number," she said. "Don't get grouchy. You're the one who feels 'rusty,' or whatever you were saying before."

"Does last night count?" I asked. I was intrigued, I have to admit.

Charlie looked thoughtful. "Yes," she decided, after a moment. "Because you were acting on a specific directive when you chatted up Kris."

"Yes, yes I was," I agreed smugly. "One target down, twenty-nine to go." I pulled my hair out of its dirty ponytail and efficiently wrapped it right back up again, trapping any stray hairs that had emerged during my vehement protest of this plan.

"Target?" Charlie asked.

"You know, like, 'target practice.' You pick a target, aim, fire. That's me." I explained.

"I love it," Charlie said, laughing.

the party room

by Morgan Burke

The party room is where all the prep school kids drink up and hook up. All you need is a fake ID and your best Juicy Couture to get in.

One night, Samantha Byrne leaves with some guy no one's ever seen before . . . and ends up dead in Central Park. Murdered gruesomely. Found at the scene of the crime: a school tie from Talcott Prep.

New York is suddenly in the grip of a raging media frenzy. And a serial killer walks amidst Manhattan's most privileged—and indulged—teens.

And the party isn't over yet. . . .
Last Call in June 2005!

Published by Simon Pulse

The books that all your mates have been talking about!

Collect all the books in the best-selling series by

cathy Hopkins

"Bridget Jones as a Teen."
—*Teen People*

the nine lives of chloe king by CELIA THOMSON

1 hero.
9 lives.
8 left.

It happened fast. Just a moment earlier, Chloe had been sitting with Amy and Paul on the observation deck atop Coit Tower in San Francisco. *What would happen if I dropped a penny from up here?* she wondered. She climbed up on the railing and dug into her jeans pocket, hunting for spare change.

That was when she fell.

As Chloe tumbled through the fog, all she could think was, *My mother will be so upset when she finds out I skipped school. . . . Maybe all that stuff about your life flashing before your eyes is just bull.*

Or maybe Chloe already knew, down in the unconscious depths of her mind, that she still had eight lives to go.

Don't miss this hot new series from Simon Pulse:

The Fallen   The Stolen   The Chosen

Published by Simon & Schuster